BLP
8/7.0

D0616265

DATE DUE

DEC 17			
FEB 17 '11			

Sudd... ...to
pound as ... ...
couldn't b... ...le
music and... ...d
the room ...

The foo... ...d
not pass i... ...es
of ghostly... ...d
Plantation... ...e on
the back o... ...s
spirit by b...

CJF   15874
Lut   Luttrell, Wanda.
      Whispers in Williamsburg

                           5,8/7.0

Please Return To:
Grace Christian School Library
M-140
616-463-5545

Be sure to read all the books
in Sarah's Journey

Home on Stoney Creek
Stranger in Williamsburg
Reunion in Kentucky
Whispers in Williamsburg
Shadows on Stoney Creek

Also Available as an Audio Book:
Home on Stoney Creek

SARAH'S JOURNEY

WHISPERS IN
WILLIAMSBURG

Wanda Luttrell

Thanks to Elisabeth Brown and Sue Reck, my editors,
for their help with the next chapter of Sarah's Journey.

Chariot Books is an imprint of Chariot Victor Publishing
Cook Communications, Colorado Springs, CO 80918
Cook Communications, Paris, Ontario
Kingsway Communications, Eastbourne, England

WHISPERS IN WILLIAMSBURG
© 1997 by Wanda Luttrell

All rights reserved. Except for brief excerpts for review purposes,
no part of this book may be reproduced or used in any form
without written permission from the publisher.

Cover design by Mary Schluchter
Cover illustration by Bill Farnsworth
Interior illustrations by John Zielinski
First printing, 1997
Printed in the United States of America
01   5 4

Contents

For my precious
little granddaughters,
Ana Victoria
and
Lidia Leigh

ChariotVICTOR

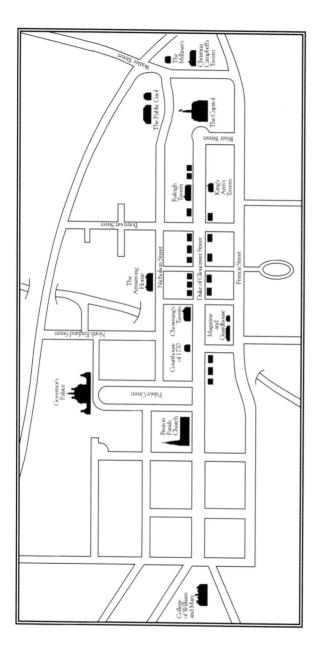

Williamsburg 1700s

Sarah Moore stopped at the end of the Palace Green and looked down Duke of Gloucester Street, where the shops and taverns of Williamsburg beckoned. Even on this gray November day, the street fairly glistened with excitement.

"Hurry, Sarah!" her eight-year-old cousin, Megan, urged, skipping backward ahead of her. "John Greenhow's store will be closed before we get there, and the milliner's, too! And Ma is going to be very displeased if we come back empty-handed!"

Sarah grimaced at the thought of her Aunt Charity's thin-lipped displeasure. "I'm coming, Meggie!" she assured her little cousin, "but it's not even noon yet, and Greenhow's store and the milliner will be open for hours!"

Quickly crossing the dusty street, Sarah climbed the steps to where Megan waited, impatiently tapping one foot on the stoop, but she couldn't resist one last glance down Duke of Gloucester Street. Though their tutor last year, the beautiful Gabrielle Gordon, had told of faraway places that made the capital city of Virginia seem like a poor village, Williamsburg still was the most exciting place Sarah had ever been, and Duke of Gloucester Street was the most exciting part of it.

Sarah noticed a crowd milling around in front of the genteel Raleigh Tavern, about three blocks down and across the street. What was going on? It was too far away to hear what the crowd was saying. Most likely, they were reading another printer's broadside about the war. America's war for independence from the tyranny of Great Britain seemed to be all the inhabitants of Williamsburg talked about these days.

The war and the Governor's Christmas Ball, Sarah reminded herself. And if she didn't get the trimming for their dresses her aunt had sent her and Meggie to buy, she guessed she and her cousins wouldn't be going.

Suddenly as eager as Megan to shop in Greenhow's store, Sarah crossed the threshold, breathing in the pungent odor of cinnamon and nutmeg, mingled with the bayberry and lemon scent of candles and soaps, and the wood shavings from the barrels of merchandise around the room.

Oh, I wish Ma could shop here! she thought. There were no stores like this in Kentucky, selling needles and pins and buttons, or rich brown sugar, or coffee and spices from the West Indies.

Megan tugged at her hand. "Look, Sarah! There are those 'licious little chocolate pearls! Though I can't imagine why they call them 'pearls.' They're bigger and flatter than pearls, and they're not white, except for some of the sweet sprinklings on top."

Sarah's gaze followed the little girl's to the bin filled with the little candies her oldest brother, Nathan, had introduced

★ Chapter One ★

her to that day, a year ago last summer, when he had left her with their Aunt Charity's family to study with her cousins. Before he had left Williamsburg to rejoin his regiment of Patriot soldiers, Nate had given her a paper of the little chocolates.

" 'Nonpareils,' Meggie," Sarah corrected. "Remember, I told you that our tutor last year explained that 'nonpareils' is a French word that means 'without equal'?"

"Could we get some, Sarah?" the little girl begged, her dark eyes wide and hopeful. "They're my absolute fav'rite! Do you think Ma would be terribly angry if we spent just a bit of her money on nonpearls?"

Sarah gave up on the word. She didn't want to think about the beautiful Gabrielle, their half-English, half-French tutor who had turned out to be a spy. "I have a little money of my own, Meggie. I'll get us some nonpareils before we leave," she promised, turning to examine other merchandise displayed around the store.

There was no sign of the young clerk who had waited on her a year ago. The last time she had seen him, he was marching with the Patriot militia on the Palace Green to the rhythm of drum and fife. Where was he now? Had he been killed by a British bullet on some lonely battlefield? Had Nate?

Quickly, Sarah turned her thoughts from battles and bullets, and completed the purchases her aunt had sent her to make, all but the ribbons for their dresses. Aunt Charity always bought her trimmings from Greenhow's if they had what she wanted, for the shopkeeper had his own boats to bring merchandise down the James River, and thus, could charge less for them. The milliner's offerings would be more expensive. But not only was Aunt Charity careful with every farthing and pound, she also was very sure of exactly what she wanted and would settle for nothing less.

"Come, Meggie," Sarah said, taking the little girl's hand to draw her away from the tempting merchandise in front of them, "we'll have to visit the milliner, after all."

As they made their way back across the street and covered the few blocks between Greenhow's and the milliner's, Sarah noticed that the crowd in front of the Raleigh had grown. Perhaps they should wander down that way and gather whatever news was available before they visited the milliner. Aunt Charity liked to keep up with current events.

Just then, a man jerked a black man up onto the steps of the tavern. He stripped his shirt down to expose the muscular chest and shoulders to the crisp November weather.

Sarah gasped as she realized what was happening. It was a slave auction, the second she had seen since she'd returned from Kentucky to Williamsburg to study.

Sarah glanced down at Megan, who was happily occupied with placing a nonpareil in her mouth and twisting the paper that held them securely around the remaining pieces.

"You want one, Sarah?" she asked.

"No, thanks, Meggie, not now," Sarah answered, hoping to get the little girl into the milliner's shop before she realized what was going on a few doors down the street.

★ Chapter One ★

Sarah knew that Uncle Ethan and Aunt Charity owned no slaves, and did not believe in slavery. They had one hired servant, sour-faced old Hester Starkey, who helped with the household chores and cooking, and one man who took care of the sheep and cattle when Uncle Ethan was away on his frequent trips on behalf of the Patriots.

"Slavery flies in the face of every principle of the Revolution," Uncle Ethan had said just the other night, as the family had finished their evening meal with dessert in the parlor.

There had been a sale that day of the slaves from a nearby estate whose owner had died, and Sarah and her cousins, Abigail and Tabitha, had come upon it in front of the courthouse on their way to the tutor's. They had stood in the street and watched in horror as the black people were auctioned off like cattle, then herded down the street behind their new owner's carriage. The girls had not been able to get it off their minds and had had many questions for their uncle and father during dinner.

"Our papers declaring our independence from Great Britain themselves state, 'All men are created equal, and endowed by their Creator with certain inalienable rights,' " Uncle Ethan had proclaimed, getting up to pace the room as he talked. "Of course, some people say that slaves are not really human, that they were not created equal and, therefore, have no rights under that law. But how can we who are risking so much in the pursuit of freedom indulge ourselves in the enslavement of any people?" he had asked.

Sarah agreed. Her best friend, Marcus, had been a slave until he was freed by Governor Dunmore's wife just before the Dunmores had fled back to England at the start of the war. And Marcus, who now was employed as the gardener at

13

the palace where Virginia's governor lived, was certainly human! He was one of the nicest and one of the wisest people Sarah ever had known.

Suddenly, Sarah saw her uncle standing at the edge of the crowd. At the same instant, he looked up and saw her and Megan on the steps of the milliner's shop. A frown creased his forehead, and he made a movement with his hand that plainly ordered her to take Megan away from there.

Sarah remembered how Megan had cried the other night as they discussed the slave auction, and how her father and mother had ended up taking her to bed with them to calm her down so they all could get to sleep.

"There's Pa!" the little girl cried out, as Sarah took her by the hand and urged her inside the milliner's. "Stop it, Sarah!" she said. "I want to see Pa!"

"No, Meggie, not now," Sarah said firmly, one eye on her uncle and his obvious concern that his young daughter not witness the spectacle about to take place before them. "We've got to get those ribbons and get back before your Ma sends sour old Hester Starkey after us!" It wasn't much of a threat, but it was the best Sarah could think of at the moment.

The little girl went with her into the shop, but she kept looking back over her shoulder the whole time Sarah was buying the ribbons. When they came out onto the stoop, Sarah was relieved to see her uncle standing there.

Quickly, he stooped and gave Meggie a hug. "What are you doing here, Sarah?" he asked over the child's head.

"We came to do some shopping for Aunt Charity, but John Greenhow's didn't have the ribbons for the dresses she is making us for the Governor's Ball," Sarah stammered, "and we had to come here to the milliner's. But we are finished now and can go home, if you wish, sir."

"Not only do I wish it, but I command it!" he said. "You know what a time we had the other night, Sarah," he said more gently.

She nodded. "Come along, Meggie," she urged. "Aunt Charity will be waiting. And I'm starved! Let's go see what old Hester has prepared for dinner. Maybe she'll serve fried chicken, and you know how you love Hester's crispy chicken!"

The little girl looked up at her with scorn in her dark eyes, so like her father's. "You know Hester never serves fried chicken for dinner, Sarah," she said.

"Well, sometimes she does when your father is home."

"Tell Charity I won't be home for dinner, girls," he said. "I've business to attend, but I plan to be back in time for supper tonight."

He patted Meggie on the head and smiled at Sarah. Then, through clenched teeth, he said, "Take her out of here, Sarah. I do not want her—nor you—to witness man's inhumanity to man."

"Uncle Ethan, hasn't the sale of slaves been outlawed in Virginia?" Sarah whispered. "I thought the legislature . . ."

"The law only forbade the importation of slaves from Africa or the West Indies," he said. "These poor people belonged to a Loyalist to the king of England who has fled for safety back to the mother country. His property is being sold to satisfy the claims of his creditors. Run along now, Sarah, and take Meggie home."

Sarah took Megan's hand and led her back the way they had come. Crossing the next street, she glanced behind her and saw that her uncle had rejoined the crowd in front of the Raleigh.

"And here they go!" she heard the auctioneer call out. Meggie struggled to turn around, but Sarah held her hand firmly, half-dragging her down the brick sidewalk and around the corner onto Palace Street.

Her thoughts were whirling. If her uncle were so set against slavery, why was he there taking part in the auction? Or, at least, he was watching it. Suddenly, Sarah wanted to go back to Duke of Gloucester Street and see the spectacle for herself, to ask questions of her uncle, to try to understand.

"Give this basket with the ribbons and her change to your ma," she told Megan, opening the gate and giving the little girl a gentle shove toward the front of the neat brick house before them.

Megan held onto the gate. "Where are you going, Sarah? Can't I go with you?"

"No, you can't!" Sarah snapped impatiently. Then, seeing the hurt look on the child's face, she gave her a quick hug. "I didn't mean to snap at you, Meggie," she apologized. "It's just that I'm in a hurry. But I'll be back in three shakes of a dead sheep's tail," she promised, leaving the little girl with a puzzled expression as she tried to figure out just how long that would be.

Sarah ran down Nicholson Street to where it intersected with Botetourt, then turned right. At Duke of Gloucester, she turned left.

The crowd at the Raleigh was quiet, listening to the silken voice of the auctioneer as he spoke of the strength and agility of the muscular black man he held by the arm on the steps of the tavern. Then he praised the weaving and household skills of a tall, thin black woman, and pointed out the beauty and the childbearing potential of the frightened-looking young girl beside her.

Why, she's surely not much older than I am! Sarah thought in horror. What if that were Sarah Moore standing on the steps of the Raleigh, being auctioned off to the highest bidder? *How would I feel?* she wondered. *How would it be to belong to somebody, to have to do whatever that somebody commanded?*

Marcus's wife, Dulcie, and his son, Sam, had belonged to a James River plantation owner who had sold them to a slave trader. Marcus had told Sarah about little Sam's sobbing as they tore him out of his father's arms and loaded him on a wagon for the journey south to the cotton plantations. He had recalled the bleak, dead look in Dulcie's dark eyes that had made him wonder if she would ever sing again. "My Dulcie could sing like a wild canary!" he had said.

Sarah smiled, remembering with satisfaction her part in rescuing Marcus's family from the Indians who had massacred their owner and his family as they tried to relocate to Kentucky. Since she and Uncle Ethan had brought Dulcie and Sam back to Marcus, his little house down in Raccoons Chase often rang with Dulcie's beautiful voice.

"Going once, going twice," the auctioneer sang out, "sold to the gentleman over here in the blue coat."

Was the auction over, so soon? Apparently so, for the crowd moved restlessly, already beginning to thin out. Then in amazement, Sarah saw her Uncle Ethan step up and begin counting money into the hand of the auctioneer! She closed her eyes tightly, then opened them, but the scene before her had not changed. After all his indignant words about slavery the other night, had her uncle just bought three slaves?

"Uncle Ethan . . . ," she began.

He looked up, a frown crossing his face and settling in his usually warm brown eyes. She couldn't be sure if he had seen her or not, but something certainly had displeased him.

Her uncle led the slaves, shuffling in the chains around their ankles, toward a wagon standing nearby which was hitched to two horses she thought she recognized from the palace stables. Then she saw that Marcus was perched in the driver's seat! Were the slaves the governor's then? Had Uncle Ethan bought them for him?

Some men joined her uncle at the wagon. Sarah recognized Governor Henry, Thomas Jefferson, and George Wythe—surely the ugliest man in all of Williamsburg, she thought, but also one of the most intelligent. All three men had visited the Armstrong house at various times.

Mr. Jefferson handed the slaves some papers, the governor nodded at Marcus, and the wagon pulled away from the curb. At the corner, instead of turning toward the palace, though, Marcus turned the horses toward the Jamestown Road.

Sarah turned back toward her uncle and found him staring at her. His face wore that "we'll discuss this later" look.

As she turned to walk away, Sarah heard a man say in a hoarse whisper, "John 3:19. Tonight."

"Darkness to light," someone else responded softly. Was it Uncle Ethan?

She threw a glance back over her shoulder and saw her uncle and Mr. Jefferson going up the steps to the Raleigh. Governor Henry got into a carriage and was driven away down the street.

As she covered the distance to Nicholson Street, Sarah's mind seethed with unanswered questions. What on earth was going on here? What did the cryptic message mean? "John 3:19, John 3:19," she repeated, determined not to forget the reference.

When she reached the Armstrong house, she went straight to Uncle Ethan's study and looked up the verse in the big black Bible he kept on his desk.

"And this is the condemnation," she read, "that light is come into the world, and men loved darkness rather than light, because their deeds were evil." Her uncle had underlined the last eleven words. What could it mean?

All through dinner and during afternoon chores, Sarah

pondered the verse and the men's whispered reference to it. Finally, as the big clock in the hall struck three o'clock, she left the house, headed for the palace gardens. Surely Marcus would be back by now, and she planned to ask him some questions. Obviously, he was involved in this strange business, if only as an obedient servant of the governor. Surely he could tell her what was happening!

If Marcus were in the gardens, though, she couldn't find him. After she had searched the entire grounds and the stables for him, she sank down on a wooden bench just beyond the sculptured hollies and boxwoods of the formal ballroom garden. She would wait until Marcus decided to come back, she resolved.

Soon her thoughts were interrupted by footsteps on the graveled paths. Then a familiar voice said, "As I've said on many occasions, I believe slavery to be repugnant to humanity!"

"You are absolutely right, Governor," Sarah heard Uncle Ethan agree.

"I admit," the governor went on, "that I own slaves, drawn along by the general inconvenience of living without them, but I have plans. . . ."

"Well, you know how I feel," a third voice interrupted. "I've fought legal battles for the right of a man to free his slaves if he so desires. Some are doing so in their last wills and testaments, but the practice never has been declared legal in Virginia, or anywhere else in America that I know of."

"I will never forget your plea before the General Court for the 'universality of human freedom,' Tom," the governor said. "It is one of the things that convinced me slavery is inconsistent with our struggles for freedom here in America."

"It's a theory held dear by George Wythe, too," Jefferson continued. "I admit that his teachings about the law and human rights have greatly influenced me, and I totally agree with him that the American struggle for independence must also abolish slavery!" he said emphatically.

"Amen!" Sarah's uncle agreed. "And I am sure you could find support for that belief in many places. John Adams of Boston says that if we allow slavery to exist in our new American states, our descendants 100 years from now will curse us for the trouble it will bring."

"I suppose even pompous bigots like Adams are entitled to be right once in a while!" Jefferson conceded.

"Oh, Adams is not such a bad sort, Tom!" the governor said, laughing. "The two of you just don't see eye-to-eye on some things."

Jefferson snorted. "On most things!" he corrected.

Sarah was more confused than ever. If these three men felt so strongly about the horrors of slavery, why had they been involved earlier today in the purchase of slaves?

"Some black men have been told that they may earn their freedom by serving in the Patriot army," the governor continued, "though there is no legal precedent to confirm it."

"Some are being sent into war by their masters as substitutes for their owners or their sons," Jefferson said. "Why, just the other day, two young black boys were sent to war by William Hogart, down on the York River, in place of his two worthless sons. Is that not the worst form of slavery, to force a man to lay his life on the line as a sacrifice for someone else? Especially when the ones whose places they are taking aren't worth shooting anyway!"

"It's been done before," Uncle Ethan said dryly, "nearly

eighteen hundred years ago in Jerusalem."

"But that was voluntary, I believe, Colonel," Jefferson pointed out, and their laughter followed them toward the palace.

Sarah sat chewing her lip. Everything the three men had said seemed to contradict their actions at the slave auction. Yet she knew these men to be of good character—truthful, honest, and trustworthy—especially her Uncle Ethan.

She got up and walked over to the canal, absently watching the white swans swim gracefully back and forth, catching insects in the water. The swans always reminded Sarah of her beautiful tutor who had been deported to France.

Sarah turned to look down toward the maze, knowing that in the fading light it would be nearly dark inside the thick planting of shrubs. The maze had been designed in a winding puzzle of paths to delight the guests of the king's governors who had ruled the colonies before the colonists declared their independence from Great Britain. But it was too close and smothery, too confusing to suit her.

She shivered, recalling the evening she had come to the maze and passed what she had thought was a shopping list from Gabrielle to Alistair Devon, the infamous British spy, the "Demon Devon" whom her uncle and the Patriots had sought to hang.

She turned her thoughts from the treacherous Gabrielle, who had turned out to be as confusing and contradictory as the maze itself. She didn't want to think her uncle was like the woman he had denounced for spying against the Patriot cause, but what could Sarah think when he said one thing and did another?

Hearing the crunch of wheels on gravel, she hurried to the stables. Surely it was Marcus, returning with the wagon that had transported the slaves.

Then she noticed that, though it did appear to be the wagon she had seen earlier, the man driving it was not Marcus. It was someone she had never seen before. And the wagon was empty. Where had they taken the slaves, and why?

"Where's Marcus?" she asked the man.

"He's gone on down to his house, missy," the black man answered, avoiding her eyes as he climbed down from his seat at the front of the wagon.

"I know where that is. Thank you," she said, turning to go.

The man reached out a hand, as though to stop her. "I wouldn't go down there, missy," he warned. "Not now."

"But why not?" she asked, puzzled. Marcus always seemed glad to see her, and so did Dulcie. The poor troubled woman had even begun to talk to Sarah about her home and family, though she never mentioned her ordeals on the cotton plantation or as a captive of the Indians.

"Mr. Marcus is . . . busy, ma'am," the man said, still avoiding her eyes. "I wouldn't go down there tonight, if I was you."

How mysterious the man was trying to be! But Sarah had no time for games.

"Thank you!" she called back over her shoulder, hurrying through the gates and into Nicholson Street. She had no intention of heeding the man's advice.

The sun was sinking behind the trees as Sarah left Botetourt Street and headed north across the fields in the general direction of Raccoons Chase. Soon she came to the dirt street that led between the rows of rough wooden houses where many of Williamsburg's black people, both free and slave, made their homes.

Most of the yards were bare dirt, but the little house with the red door where Marcus lived had a good stand of grass. Frost, though, had killed the bright flowers that usually lined the walk Marcus had built of broken bricks salvaged from the pile of discards at the palace.

Sarah knocked at the red door and stood waiting on the stoop, listening to the wind whispering through the cedars and rattling the dry oak leaves that still clung determinedly to their branches. She shivered and pulled her shawl closer around her, wishing she had her heavy cloak.

It was a good evening to be inside a snug little house in

front of a glowing fireplace, she thought, breathing in the pleasant, homey odor of wood smoke from the chimneys around her.

She knocked again. A furtive movement from inside the house convinced her someone was there.

"Marcus?" she called softly. "It's me. Sarah. Let me in! I need to talk with you!"

The door opened a crack. Through it, she could see a dark eye peering out at her. That certainly wasn't Marcus! It was likely Dulcie, afraid to open the door.

Dulcie hadn't been able to speak when they first rescued her. Sarah recalled her eerie, wordless wailing as she rocked back and forth in a straight-backed chair, a blank look in her eyes. Now, her eyes were bright and lively, and she had recovered her speech. She even sang sometimes, when there weren't too many people around.

What's wrong with her now? Sarah wondered. "Dulcie! It's me! Sarah!" she called softly to the woman. "Let me in!"

The door opened about half way, and Sarah squeezed around it. Immediately, Dulcie shut it and slid the bar across it.

"What's wrong, Dulcie?" she asked. "Why are you so afraid again?"

The woman stared at her out of wide, solemn eyes, but gave no answer.

Sarah looked around the room that served as parlor, bedroom, and kitchen, not unlike the one-room cabin her own family had shared on the banks of Stoney Creek their first year in Kentucky.

A wooden bedstead covered with a faded patchwork quilt filled one corner, with the washstand holding its cracked pitcher and bowl beside it. A rocking chair and a straight-backed chair sat facing each other in front of the brick fireplace, where a small iron kettle hung from a crane over the fire. A long-handled wooden spoon and a dish towel dangled from square iron nails driven into the edge of the mantel. Two mismatched chairs pushed under a small table completed the room's furnishings.

Sarah took a deep breath. The room smelled of fresh, warm cornbread, with a hint of bacon grease. Her stomach growled, reminding her that she had not gone home for supper.

"Dulcie, where's Marcus?" she asked.

Dulcie shook her head, her tight white curls trembling. "You don't want to go down there, Miss Sarah!" she whispered.

"Down where, Dulcie? What's wrong? Where is your husband?" Something was wrong, and Sarah was becoming alarmed. She took the woman by the shoulders and shook her a little. "Where's Marcus?" she demanded.

Dulcie stared at the floor. "Church," she muttered, so low Sarah barely heard. "He be at church."

"Church?" Sarah questioned. "But this isn't Sunday!" Sarah knew Marcus and his family sat with the other black people of Williamsburg in the north balcony of the big brick church she and her uncle's family attended, but services were held only on Sunday morning, and on Good Friday and Christmas Day. There was nothing going on at Bruton Parish Church this plain dark evening in November.

Dulcie raised her eyes to Sarah's. "Don't go down there, Miss Sarah!" she begged.

"I have to see Marcus, Dulcie," she insisted. Her questions about the slave auction could wait until morning, she supposed, but something had frightened Dulcie greatly. She had to find out what it was.

Dulcie's eyes rolled fearfully. Finally, she pointed down toward the woods. "He be down there, Miss Sarah. In the last cabin next to the woods," she whispered. "And he'll be angry at Dulcie for telling!"

"Marcus wouldn't hurt you for anything on this earth, Dulcie, and you know it!" Sarah patted the woman's shoulder reassuringly. "Anyway, I won't tell him how I found out," she promised, reaching for the bar across the door and pulling it back.

"You don't want to be caught down there, Miss Sarah!" Dulcie said, clutching Sarah's forearm. "I be warning you!"

Sarah patted her on the shoulder again, pulled her arm from Dulcie's grasp, and went outside. Behind her, she heard the door shut and the bar slide into place.

It was completely dark now, and Sarah had to pick her way carefully by the light of a pale November moon that spilled through the naked tree limbs and silvered the unpainted boards of the houses around her. Then the road ended.

Off in the woods, a screech owl called, his eerie cry carried on the wind to Raccoons Chase. Sarah tucked her shawl around her arms, took a deep breath, and plunged down a narrow path that led across the meadow to a dark square of cabin just this side of the woods.

The faint flickering of candlelight outlined the one shuttered window visible from the side. From inside the cabin, Sarah could hear a deep, unrecognizable rumbling, like the sound of bees buzzing in a hive. She looked around for something to climb on, but there was nothing. Quietly, she made her way around the cabin to what appeared to be the only door. It was shut.

The rumbling stopped, then began again. She was close enough now to realize it was singing. She could distinguish the words: "Oh, God, our help in ages past, our hope in days to come!" There was something strange about the singing, though. Then she knew what it was. There were no women's voices mingled with the deep basses and high tenors of the men inside the cabin.

Suddenly a hand grasped her by the wrist, and she uttered a small scream. Then her arm was twisted painfully up behind her back, and she was pushed toward the door of the cabin. Her captor kicked open the door and shoved her inside.

Sarah blinked in the glare of what she soon realized was really the very dim light of one flickering candle, burning on a crude table at one end of the room. She looked around the square, dirt-floored room, and saw that a dozen or so black men sat on backless benches, all of them staring at her, their song cut short by her entrance.

"Miss Sarah?" It was Marcus's voice, and she turned toward it, wincing as pain shot up her twisted arm. Marcus wouldn't let them hurt her. She was sure of that! She trembled in relief.

"Let her go!" he commanded, and instantly, her arm was released. Her former captor moved around her and over to sit on one of the benches, and Sarah recognized the man who had driven the wagon back to the palace stables earlier in the evening, the one who had warned her not to come down here.

"Now, missy, you tell Marcus what you're doing here," Marcus demanded sternly, moving over to stand in front of her.

"I . . . I was looking for you, Marcus," she stammered,

★ Chapter Three ★

unable at the moment to remember why.

Marcus patted her reassuringly on the arm, as she had done to Dulcie only moments ago. "You get on back home now, honey," he said kindly. "This is no place for the likes of you!"

She glanced around the room again. Dark faces stared at her from every bench, hostile faces with angry eyes. There wasn't a woman or a child in the room. Obviously, this was no ordinary church meeting. Were the slaves planning a rebellion? She had heard terrible stories of such things in other places, where slaves ravaged and burned the plantations and killed their owners.

If so, though, why was Marcus a part of it? He had not been a slave since the Dunmores had fled back to England at the start of the war.

"I reckon somebody better walk home with you, Miss Sarah," Marcus said. "This is no night for you to be wandering around the outskirts of Williamsburg all by yourself!"

"I think we're through here for now," a familiar voice said from the shadows behind the candle. In amazement, Sarah watched as her uncle stood and walked around the table. "I'll see Sarah home," he promised Marcus, taking her by the elbow and urging her firmly toward the door.

"Hold on there!" someone cried. "How do we know but what she overheard everything?"

"Yeah, she may have been out there eavesdropping the whole time!" another voice added.

Uncle Ethan looked at her questioningly, and Sarah shook her head. "I couldn't see or hear anything but some singing," she answered. "I just wanted to find Marcus to . . ."

"Obviously, she knows nothing, gentlemen," Uncle Ethan assured them. "I'll just see her home, and we'll be about our business."

"How do we know she's telling the truth?" the first man questioned, getting to his feet.

Sarah's heart sank, as several of the men joined him, their eyes dark and unreadable.

"What if she sounds the alarm before—" the man began.

"Gentlemen, this is my niece, Sarah. I will take her home to my house, where she will stay the rest of the night. Won't you, Sarah?" he asked ominously. She swallowed hard and nodded. "She will do our cause no harm. I give you my word. Is that not good enough for you?"

The men shuffled their feet and dropped their gaze to the floor.

"The girl got here only moments before I brought her inside," her former captor said. "I followed her all the way from the Chase. And I don't think we need to be questioning the word of a man who is probably the best friend we have in this old world."

★ Chapter Three ★

"I'm sorry, Colonel Armstrong, sir," the first man apologized quickly. "If you say the girl will do us no harm, then I am willing to take your word for it."

The other men murmured agreement, and one by one, they sat down.

Uncle Ethan nodded. "All right, men. Remember John 3:19. You know what to do," he added as he led Sarah through the door and into the darkness.

There it was again, that mysterious reference to the Bible verse she had looked up in the Bible on her uncle's desk.

"Uncle Ethan," she panted, trying to keep up with his long stride as he all but pulled her across the meadow and onto the dirt road of the Chase, "what is John 3:19?"

"A Bible verse," he answered tersely.

"I know that, Uncle Ethan, but . . ."

He stopped so suddenly that she nearly ran over him. "Sarah, curiosity killed the cat, I'm told, and you have more curiosity than half a dozen cats!"

"But . . . ," she protested.

"But nothing!" he said sternly, shaking the arm he still held in his iron grasp. "John 3:19 is a Bible verse, and the less you know about why it is being whispered around Williamsburg, the better off you will be!"

Sarah let him lead her down the dirt track and onto Botetourt Street. Soon they were walking rapidly down Nicholson Street to the gate of the Armstrong house.

"Get inside where you belong, Sarah," he ordered, opening the gate for her. "And please, stay there!"

"Yes, sir," she said meekly. "I'm sorry, sir. I . . ."

She heard him sigh. "You are always sorry, Sarah," he said wearily, shutting the gate behind her.

Sarah hurried up the brick walk to the Armstrong's front door. As she reached for the latch, the door opened.

"Where have you been, Sarah?" Abigail scolded. "We've finished supper, and . . ."

Sarah turned to look back at her uncle, but he had disappeared into the darkness.

"Come on in and hear the great news!" Abigail chattered breathlessly, pulling Sarah inside, across the entry, and into the dining room. "Ma has found us a music and dancing teacher!"

"You are very late, Sarah," Aunt Charity greeted her with that familiar thin-lipped smile that did not quite reach her pale blue eyes.

Aunt Charity looks so much like Ma, Sarah thought, *except for her blond hair.* But her cold expression held no resemblance to the warmth and love she was used to encountering in her mother.

"I . . . was with Uncle Ethan, Aunt Charity," Sarah

answered truthfully. She knew her aunt was waiting for further explanation, but what could she say?

Finally, Aunt Charity said, "I will talk with Ethan when he returns," she warned. "Meanwhile, go wash your hands, Sarah, and Tabitha, ask Hester to bring Sarah something to eat."

Sarah ran to the kitchen to do as her aunt suggested, then hurried back to the table, drying her hands on her skirt. Aunt Charity frowned, but said nothing.

"The music teacher, Ma!" Abigail urged. "Tell her about Señor Alfredo Alvarez! It's so exciting!" she continued to Sarah. "He has come here from Spain to live at Pleasantwood Plantation and teach the Woodard children to dance, sing, and play instruments. And Ma has arranged for us to take lessons from him every Friday afternoon!"

"But that's tomorrow!" Sarah interrupted. "And isn't Pleasantwood Plantation down on the James River? That's a long walk from here. How will we get there?"

Aunt Charity's smile held real amusement this time. "It's over an hour by carriage, my dear," she said. "Marcus's son, Sam, will drive you in our carriage. It's all arranged. I want you girls to be the belles of the ball at the Governor's Palace next month," she added, with another genuine smile.

"I am already the best dancer in Williamsburg," Abigail put in smugly.

The sad thing was, Sarah thought, her conceited cousin probably was right. She danced with a grace and skill that few of Williamsburg's ladies could match, she would guess, and she played the harpsichord equally well. But Sarah wasn't jealous of Abigail. Music, dancing, and fashion were 'Gail's forte. Tabby was the accomplished seamstress, housekeeper, and hostess. And Sarah? she wondered. What was she?

"You are my star pupil," Gabrielle had said to her more than once. And, of the three of them, she supposed that was true. She had devoured the lessons Gabrielle had taught her in Latin, in the literature and customs of the peoples of the world, in the fascinating histories of places like Paris, London, and Rome. That was why Gabrielle had called her "star pupil."

Uncle Ethan, she thought suddenly, would be more likely to say she was his star troublemaker! He was always either rescuing her from or punishing her for some impossible situation she had created with her stubborn determination to do things her own way. And she thought she had left all that behind her when she had given her life to God on the trail back in Kentucky!

"Isn't it exciting, Sarah?" Abigail asked, dancing around the room.

What was 'Gail talking about? she wondered for a moment; then she remembered the music and dancing lessons. "Of course, it's exciting, 'Gail!" she said. "I can hardly wait to see Pleasantwood Plantation! You and Tabitha have told me so many tales of its grandeur."

"We will discontinue your lessons with Miss Jamison on Fridays," Aunt Charity explained, as Hester came in with a steaming bowl and a cloth-covered basket. She threw Sarah a sour look, but Sarah smiled at her warmly, suddenly ravenously hungry.

Sarah spooned up a bit of lamb stew and followed it with a piece of Hester's flaky biscuits that couldn't even be ruined by being warmed over. Then she began to eat hungrily.

"I don't think it's a bit fair for all of you to go off on such 'citing 'ventures and leave me here at home by myself," Megan pouted. "After all, there's only so many things you can do with one little cat to play with," she added plaintively.

A look of indignation crossed the little girl's face as they all laughed.

"Your day will come, dear," Aunt Charity said, giving her youngest daughter a comforting hug.

Sarah smiled and winked at Meggie, but the little girl glared back at her.

Sarah then turned her attention to her cousins' excited babbling about tomorrow and what they would wear and what they would do on their visit to Pleasantwood Plantation. Soon, they had exhausted the subject and themselves, and went to bed without protest at Aunt Charity's first suggestion.

Sarah lay in the big bed beside Megan, who lay stiffly on the far rail for all of five minutes before she went sound asleep and rolled back to her usual position in the middle of the deep featherbed.

Sarah loved this feisty little cousin as much as she loved her own little brother, Jamie, and baby sister, Elizabeth. Meggie was a whole lot like she was, but Sarah hoped the little girl would not be quite so headstrong and get in as much trouble as she always seemed to manage to do. She hoped . . . but it had been a long day, and Sarah, herself, was soon fast asleep.

The entire household was astir before the sun rose on Friday. As soon as they had put away a batch of Hester's pancakes, Aunt Charity set the girls to tidying the house. They would be leaving for Pleasantwood Plantation right after the midday meal, and with only Hester Starkey to help with the cooking and cleaning, the sweeping, dusting, and tidying chores fell to Tabitha, who loved them, and to Abigail and Sarah, who tolerated them.

Sarah didn't mind helping out too much, though. She had always helped Ma at home, and she and Ma had had no Hester to help them do anything. They had done it all!

What was Ma doing right now? she wondered, as she dried the last of the pretty flowered dishes and put them back in the dining room cupboard. Sarah tried not to remember that the dishes had been her ma's before she had given them to Aunt Charity. Ma had cherished those dishes, which her own mother had given her on her wedding day, but she had been afraid they would be broken on the rough journey through the wilderness to Kentucky and had given them to her sister.

Sarah wished Ma could have pretty things again, like they had in Miller's Forks before Pa moved them to Kentucky. She wished she could have a nice brick house like this one, with polished floors instead of splintery half logs, and with real glass windows with damask curtains like Aunt Charity's, instead of paper greased with bear fat and covered with rough wooden shutters.

Pa kept promising that "someday" they would have all those things again, that Kentucky would be as modern and cultured as Virginia, but Sarah just couldn't imagine it as anything but an untamed wilderness.

"Sarah, I want you to run down to York Street and tell Miss Jamison that we won't be needing her services on Fridays for a while," Aunt Charity said, as Sarah put the last of the dusted figurines back on the mantel in the parlor.

Glad to be free of the household chores, Sarah grabbed her cloak, threw it around her shoulders against the early morning cold, and headed down Nicholson Street. She turned right onto Botetourt, then left onto Francis Street, which she followed all the way past the end of Waller, where

★ Chapter Four ★

Gabrielle had lived and run her millinery shop. At the end of York Street was the Nicholson house, where their new tutor leased a room.

Each morning when Miss Jamison arrived, Aunt Charity had Hester fix the tutor a cup of hot tea and a muffin or some other pastry. She knew Miss Jamison had no kitchen and was dependent on the Nicholsons' goodwill for anything more than a kettle on her hearth. Would the loss of a day's pay each week hurt Miss Jamison's meager finances? Sarah wondered, as she knocked on the door.

"It will give me one more day to work in Nicholsons' shop," Miss Jamison said, with a thin little smile of resignation. She pushed her nose-perched glasses up with one hand, smoothing her mousy brown hair with the other. "You know, I clerk there when I'm not tutoring. It helps with the rent."

She promised to see them on Monday, and went back to what Sarah was sure must be a bleak little existence in a bleak little room. Poor Miss Jamison, she thought. There were no silk dresses or exciting stories in her life.

All at once, Sarah decided to walk back by way of Waller Street. She had avoided that street since her return to Williamsburg. "But it's closer to cut down Waller straight to Nicholson," she told herself. Besides, to be honest, she found that she really did want to see Gabrielle's house again.

The little brown house with its bright blue door seemed empty, but Sarah found it filled with memories. She had spent so many happy hours there with Gabrielle and her cousins, learning all the things dull Miss Jamison taught, but in more pleasant ways.

Then there had been those precious hours she had spent alone with Gabrielle, studying hard on advanced subjects, but with the hours flying by so that she was always amazed when

Gabrielle reminded her it was time to go home.

Sarah remembered the old tabby cat on the hearth with her litter of kittens, Megan's Tiger among them. Where was she now, the cat that Gabrielle had said reminded her of Tabitha, "always content to sit on her own hearth and purr over her own things and people"? Had she made her way to some other hearth where she was busy with other kittens? And was Gabrielle busy with young French girls, telling them about America and the girls she had tutored there, as she taught them all the social graces?

Sarah could close her eyes and picture the little tea table set so elegantly for Tabitha, Abigail, and her to learn to pour tea to the perfection their charming tutor expected.

Suddenly the picture came into her mind of Alistair Devon sitting at that table copying her uncle's papers that she had let Gabrielle talk her into bringing him. If he hadn't been caught, many Patriots—possibly even her own brother Nathan—might have been killed because of the secret knowledge he would have passed to the British.

Sarah blinked away threatening tears. Would she ever be able to remember the good times and forget the pain? She had told Gabrielle that she forgave her, but she could not forget!

"I've made so many mistakes!" she whispered remorsefully.

And it was a mistake to come here today, she thought, turning away from the little house that was so filled with memories, wiping futilely with her hands at the tears that spilled down her cheeks.

"It's a beautiful afternoon for a drive," Tabitha said, as they rolled along the well-traveled road beside the James River in the Armstrong carriage.

"The waters of heaven must look like that!" Sarah breathed, unable to take her eyes off the river. "I've never seen such blue water!"

"What color are the rivers in Kentucky?" Tabitha asked.

"The Kentucky is green most of the time, except when it's flooded, and then it's a muddy brown. But even the Ohio is not this kind of blue. I've never seen water like this!"

"It's just an old river, Sarah," Abigail said. "Don't carry on so!"

Sarah studied her cousin for a moment, then decided it was no use trying to explain. Abigail simply had no interest in rivers, or trees, or even flowers, except as adornments for hair or dress.

"I wonder if this old last-year's dress is fine enough to

wear to Pleasantwood Plantation?" Abigail worried aloud, smoothing the skirt of her pink Sunday dress with both hands. "I'm sure the Misses Woodard wear silk every day of the week."

"Our dresses are silk, 'Gail," Tabitha pointed out, as they turned onto a tree-lined avenue. "Of course, they are the only silk ones we have, but we aren't here to pay a social call, anyway. We're here to study with the music master. What does it matter what we wear? So long as we are clean and decent looking," she added primly, so like Aunt Charity that Sarah laughed aloud.

Abigail gasped, and they turned to look at her, then followed her gaze to the tall brick house that had appeared before them.

"Look at the front of that house!" Sarah exclaimed.

"I'd hate to have to dust all those rooms," Tabitha said, even her domestic tendencies overwhelmed by the thought of the rooms full of furniture that surely lay behind the rows upon rows of windows.

"I think this is the back of the house," Abigail said. "I seem to remember sitting on a verandah overlooking the river at the front when we were here before."

"I can see why!" Sarah said. "The view is spectacular!"

"Many of the older houses were built facing the rivers, just as our house faces the street," Tabitha commented. "The rivers were the main highways of Virginia in those days."

Sarah nodded. As a veteran of both overland and river travel, she knew how much easier it was to travel on the smooth surface of a river than through a wilderness, provided the river went where the traveler wanted to go.

Sam swung the carriage halfway around a semicircular drive and pulled up beside a stone mounting block. He got down to help the girls out of the carriage.

"You be here to pick us up in an hour and a half, Sam," Tabitha cautioned, and Sarah was reminded again of Aunt Charity.

Sam nodded, tipped his hat, and climbed back into the driver's seat to take the carriage to the stable area.

The girls climbed the stone steps, and Tabitha lifted the heavy lion's head door knocker and let it fall. Instantly, they were admitted to a spacious hallway by a butler dressed in a spotless black suit and white knee stockings.

He bowed slightly. "You are here for the music lessons?" he queried. They nodded, too awed by the huge hallway and elegant rooms to speak. They followed the butler up a long, winding stairway to the third floor, where the music room stretched along what Sarah was sure must be at least half the length of the house. It contained a harpsichord, music stands, and dozens of dainty gilt chairs, arranged in rows and around the sides of the room.

Abigail walked over to one of several tall windows, draped in deep red velvet. "This is the front," she whispered, pointing below them to where green lawns ran all the way to the incredibly blue waters of the James.

"Ah, señoritas!" a soft voice exclaimed behind them. "You are here! Come, let us introduce ourselves. I am Señor Alfredo Alvarez of Madrid, Spain." He took Abigail's hand, bent low and kissed it, then Tabitha's and Sarah's, in turn. "And you are the Señoritas Armstrong, no?"

"No," Sarah said. "I am Sarah Moore of . . ." She hesitated, then raised her chin a notch. ". . . of Stoney Creek, Kentucky. And these are my cousins, Tabitha and Abigail Armstrong of Williamsburg, Virginia."

"Ah, but you are staying at the Armstrong house in Williamsburg, are you not, Sarita? It is a long drive from Kentucky to Pleasantwood Plantation I think!" He laughed at his joke, and Tabitha and Abigail laughed with him.

Sarah nodded curtly. *What had he called her?* Sarita? "My name is Sarah," she corrected. "Sarah Moore."

He smiled, and his swarthy skin crinkled around a generous mouth and bright, dark eyes. "Sarita. In Spanish it simply makes an endearment of your name," he explained, "a 'dear little Sarah.' "

Sarah studied the small, wiry man as he turned to her cousins. His appearance was impeccable, from his curled, shoulder-length black hair tied back with ribbon, to the silver buckles of his shiny black slippers. He wore the fashionable white ruffled shirt, fancy vest, and black knee breeches ending in white stockings that the men of Virginia were wearing these days, and every move he made indicated the tight muscle control of a dancer. Sarah expected him to twirl in an impromptu ballet at any moment.

She looked at her cousins. Abigail hung on his words, her eyes worshipful. Even Tabitha seemed fascinated by this Señor Alfredo Alvarez, in spite of her devotion to Seth Coler, a young militiaman she had determined to marry, though he was not yet aware of her intentions.

Something about Señor Alvarez, though, made Sarah uncomfortable. But maybe it was just that her experience with foreigners had been less than perfect, she thought, recalling Gabrielle and her Demon Devon.

"You may call me Señor Alfredo," he pronounced. "And now let us see what you beautiful ladies can do in music and the dance. You first, Señorita Tabitha," he suggested.

Tabitha blushed from the roots of her hair down into the neck of her gown, but, as he began to play a tune on the harpsichord, she moved to the music in a credible, if unin-spired, half minuet.

Then he turned to Sarah, who suddenly felt awkward and ignorant. "Señor . . . ah . . . Alfredo," she said, "I have had only a few dance lessons from our former tutor, but I am a willing pupil." She sank into the curtsy Gabrielle had spent so many hours teaching them. "I hope I will be able to learn the minuet before the Governor's Ball next month!" she added fervently.

He smiled and nodded. "You have the necessary grace, señorita. If Señor Alfredo cannot teach you, Sarita, no one can!" Then he reached out his hand to Abigail, who all but swooned toward him in a curtsy of which even Gabrielle would have approved. "I have saved you for last, Señorita Abigail, because I can see by your movements that you are a dancer. Come, show Alfredo!"

Abigail gave him a besotted smile, then began to dance.

As she twirled and dipped across the room, it was obvious that Señor Alfredo was correct in his assessment. She was a dancer to her very bones, just as Tabitha was a homemaker and Sarah was . . . *what?* she wondered again. *A scholar? Hardly!* she thought. Yet, Gabrielle had called her "my star pupil."

Sarah sighed. It was certain, even as they showed their skill–or in Sarah's and Tabitha's cases, lack of it—on the harpsichord, who would receive the designation of "star pupil" from the music master!

Oh, well, Sarah thought, that was exactly as she had expected. She had to give her otherwise empty-headed cousin her due. Abigail was a superb dancer and musician, just as Tabitha was an accomplished housekeeper and seamstress. Maybe someday, she would find her own niche in the world.

Sarah remembered teaching the Reynolds girls in the fort at Harrodstown. They had learned from her, and she thought it had been a pleasant experience for them as well as for her. Maybe her calling was to teach. If so, she had to find some way to get more instruction than poor Miss Jamison was able to offer.

Meanwhile, she had to get through these music and dancing lessons without making any more of a fool of herself than she must. She was relieved when this lesson was over, and Señor Alfredo rang for the butler to escort them downstairs.

No one else came to greet them or to bid them good day, so they left the house, hearing the big doors shut discreetly but firmly behind them.

Sam was waiting out back with the carriage as Tabitha had commanded. He helped them to their seats and drove

44

off down the avenue of trees.

"Isn't he wonderful?" Tabitha sighed.

"Sam?" Sarah asked, pretending she did not know the subject of Tabitha's praise. "Oh, he's just the plain old garden variety carriage driver, I would say."

"No, silly! Señor Alfredo!" Tabitha corrected. "He's so suave, so debonair, as Gabrielle would say. He's just the most . . ."

"Ah, Seth, I love you!" Sarah sang, throwing her hands into the air in a melodramatic gesture of undying love.

Tabitha glared at her. "That's different!" she insisted.

"I don't know, Tabby," Sarah teased mercilessly. "I saw you blush when Señor Alfredo took your hand. I think Seth is in danger of losing his bride-to-be before he even knows he has one. What do you think, 'Gail?"

"Hmmmmm?" Abigail answered dreamily.

"You two are impossible!" Sarah declared. She poked her head out the carriage window and called to Sam to stop the horses.

"What is it, Miss Sarah?" he asked, as he quickly pulled the carriage over to the side of the road. "Is something wrong?"

Sarah jumped down, climbed up the wheel, and settled herself on the driver's seat beside him. "Drive on, Sam!" she ordered.

"Miss Sarah!" he whispered indignantly. "You mustn't ride up here like a common servant! What would Colonel Armstrong say?"

"My uncle believes in equality for all mankind," she answered sassily. "Anyway, I need someone to talk to who has some sense. It looks to me like you're the only one around."

"All right, miss, but you're gonna get us both in trouble!"

Sarah laughed, feeling good for the first time since they had entered that awful music room. But she supposed she would have to endure the lessons. She didn't want to be pointed out at the ball as that "clumsy, uncouth yahoo from the wilderness."

"That's where Ma and I used to live," Sam interrupted her thoughts, pointing toward a large plantation on their left.

Sarah recalled Marcus telling her how he had walked out to visit his family on weekends, how little Sam had helped him in the garden, saving the fishing worms for their trips to the river after chores were done. "Were you happy there, Sam?" she asked.

He stared ahead at the road. "I don't know, Miss Sarah," he answered finally. "I was so young then. I remember doing things with Pa, and Ma singing as she worked. I guess I was as happy as a little slave boy can be. Before the trader came."

Sarah patted his hand. "I know, Sam. But you're free now, and your life down in the Chase is good, isn't it?"

He nodded. "Yes, ma'am. And Pa's got me this job at the palace, learning all about horses and vehicles from the head driver. It's a good opportunity, Miss Sarah, for the likes of me."

"That's great, Sam!" she commended. "But you can just call me 'Sarah.'"

He rolled his dark eyes at her. "Oh, no, ma'am! It's just not proper, Miss Sarah!"

"Sam's got more sense than you have, Sarah!" Tabitha scolded from inside the carriage. "Get back in here where you belong before you disgrace us all!"

Sarah laughed. "Oh, well, if you'll stop again, Sam, I'll save the family reputation!"

As she climbed down and back into the carriage, she

＊ Chapter Five ＊

could feel Sam's relief, as well as Tabitha's. Abigail still was in that world of her own, and had no knowledge of Sarah's disgracing them.

Suddenly the carriage swerved, and Sam struggled to control the horses. Sarah looked up to see another carriage bearing down upon them, the driver whipping his horses mercilessly. They could hear the man's cruel laughter as he passed.

"Whoa!" Sam called. He pulled over to the side of the road and stopped. He took out a handkerchief and wiped his face.

"What's going on?" Abigail cried, her face white with fear.

"That man tried to run us down!" Tabitha said indignantly.

"It was him," Sam said. "I'll never forget that red face and those mean, narrow eyes! And the three-crown mark on the carriage door is the mark of Basil Burwick, the man who sold my ma and me!"

I'm telling Aunt Charity as soon as we get home and Uncle Ethan as soon as he gets in," Sarah vowed. "That man is a menace!"

"Oh, Sarah, don't!" Abigail begged. "Ma will stop us from going to Pleasantwood Plantation. She will say the road is too dangerous!"

"I'm afraid 'Gail's right, Sarah," Tabitha said. "You know how Ma is about our safety."

"Something needs to be done about that man!" Sarah insisted.

"But Ma will never allow us on the Jamestown Road again!" Abigail wailed. "Our dancing and music instruction will be over!"

"We likely will never meet up with that man on the road again anyway," Tabitha put in reasonably, "but we'll never convince Ma of that. Think about it, Sarah—Pleasantwood Plantation or Miss Jamison on Fridays?"

"All right," Sarah conceded, as Sam stopped the carriage in front of the Armstrong house and helped the girls down from it. "I will tell Uncle Ethan as soon as he comes home and ask him not to mention it to Aunt Charity. But that man cannot be allowed to continue to threaten lives and abuse horses that way!"

"There's probably nothing Pa can do about it, Sarah," Tabitha pointed out. "We weren't hurt, and terrible as it is, there is no law against a man whipping his own horses."

Sarah knew her cousin was right, but she was so angry, she wanted to horsewhip the man herself. She hoped Uncle Ethan would do it for her.

He wasn't in the house when they went inside, though. Aunt Charity had not seen him since early last evening.

"I'm a little concerned about him," she confided, "but I suppose he's off on one of his . . . errands. He usually tells me he's going, though. The last thing he said last evening was that he would be home late."

"Something unexpected probably came up, Ma," Tabitha comforted her. "You know how important his work is and how impossible to predict."

Aunt Charity nodded and patted Tabitha's hand. "Yes, dear, I know," she said, but Sarah thought she sounded unconvinced.

Sarah was worried about her uncle herself. He was involved in so many Patriot endeavors, in danger much of the time. There was nothing she could do about it, though, except wait, like the rest of the family, and pray for his safe return.

Aunt Charity held supper an hour past the usual time, but, as darkness began to fall, she had Hester serve it. They ate in near silence, even Megan speaking only to ask someone to pass a dish. Sarah hardly knew what they ate.

After supper, they went into the parlor. Tabitha picked up her embroidery, and Abigail sat down at the harpsichord, but she merely picked out notes with one finger.

Megan went over to sit beside her mother, burying her head in her lap. Sarah heard her sniff a couple of times. Her eyes met Aunt Charity's worried glance over the little girl's head.

"Come, Meggie, and I'll tell you about Malinda, the black woman from Barbados who healed my ma and little sister, Elizabeth, back at the fort called Harrodstown."

As Sarah talked to entertain her little cousin, she found herself longing to see her family again. She was convinced that her ma and little Elizabeth would have died if it hadn't been for the slave woman Malinda, with her island accent, her drum, and her strange healing powers.

"God sometimes be working in mysterious ways, missy," Malinda had told her, "and if He see fit to use Malinda for one of His miracles, why not?"

"She could walk just like an Indian," Sarah said now to Meggie.

"But, Sarah, I don't know how an Indian walks," the little girl protested.

"Oh, Meggie, there are several Indians here in Williamsburg. Someone gave money to the College of William and Mary to enable the Indians to get a good education, become Christians, and go back to their tribes to convert them," Tabitha said.

"But I've never paid any attention to how they walk!" Megan insisted.

Sarah laughed. "Well, Malinda could walk just like your cat, Tiger, then," she said. "She would come up behind me and say something in my ear, and I would be scared out of three years' growth because I hadn't even known she was around! One night, when the Indians were out there in the woods all around us, I saw Malinda sneak out of the fort with a bucket in her hand, and I followed her. She was meeting Marcus's wife, Dulcie, in the woods with food and . . ."

Outside in the street, the sentry called, "Nine o'clock, and all's well!"

Almost immediately, there was a knock at the back door. All of them jumped to their feet, sewing, music, and stories forgotten.

"Sit down, girls," Aunt Charity ordered, as she walked quickly into the kitchen.

Sarah heard the kitchen door open and Aunt Charity exclaim, "Ethan! Oh, dear Lord, help us!"

Unable to sit there, the girls ran through the dining room and crowded into the kitchen doorway.

Sarah saw her uncle, supported by Marcus and another black man she did not know, trying to smile at Aunt Charity from beneath a bloody bandage around his head. Then he seemed to just crumple up and sink to the floor.

"Get him upstairs to bed, men," Aunt Charity commanded briskly. "Hester, get me some hot water, that bottle of lavender water, and clean bandages," she said over her shoulder, as she followed the men upstairs, carrying Uncle Ethan between them like a sack of cornmeal.

Megan began to cry, and Tabitha went to put an arm around her, murmuring to her comfortingly, though she kept throwing worried glances toward the stairs.

"I knew it! I just knew it!" Abigail fumed. "Why does Pa have to be so involved in everything the Patriots do? Why can't he just stay home and mind his own business? Then he wouldn't be hurt!" She burst into tears.

Sarah took the basin of water from Hester, who was juggling the lavender water and bandages, too, and followed her up the stairs.

When she entered her aunt and uncle's bedroom, she saw Uncle Ethan lying unconscious against the pillows, his face as pale as the pillow cases. His shirt had been removed, exposing various cuts across his arms and chest.

Oh, God, please don't let Uncle Ethan die! Sarah prayed silently.

Aunt Charity took the basin of water and began to bathe his face. She removed the bandage, and Sarah gasped as she saw the size and depth of the cut across his forehead.

Her aunt began to bathe gently around its edges, then filled it with the lavender water. Her uncle didn't even flinch. Obviously, he was deeply unconscious.

Aunt Charity padded the wound. "That should stop the bleeding temporarily," she said, as she began to treat the lesser wounds on his arms and chest.

"Marcus, what happened?" Sarah asked.

"Miss Sarah, it's best if none of you know much about it," he said softly. "The colonel has been cut with a sword, Mrs. Armstrong," he said to Aunt Charity. "Let's just say we were waylaid by bandits on the Jamestown Road."

"The Jamestown Road?" Aunt Charity repeated, glancing quickly at Sarah. "Why the girls went over that way just this afternoon to Pleasantwood Plantation! Your son drove them," she explained. "They're taking music and dancing lessons there."

Marcus nodded. "I wouldn't worry, ma'am, if they're traveling in the afternoon. The girls should be perfectly safe in the daylight. Just keep them home at night. You know, the

★ Chapter Six ★

Bible says that men love darkness rather than light because their deeds are evil."

"John 3:19!" Sarah breathed.

Marcus turned to study her seriously for a moment. Then he turned back to Aunt Charity. "If you need me, Mrs. Armstrong, just send for me and Marcus will come running. I think the good colonel will be all right. He just needs rest and some nourishing food to rebuild his blood."

He turned to go, then turned back. "He's a good man, Mrs. Armstrong," he said, "one beloved by many people, and surely by God Himself."

He turned quickly then, and Sarah thought she saw a hint of moisture in his dark eyes. He motioned for the other man to follow him. "I'll stop by tomorrow to see if you need anything," he promised as he left the room.

"Thank you, Marcus," Aunt Charity said. "Hester, get me a needle and thread. You can go downstairs with the other girls now, Sarah," her aunt added. "Thank you for helping."

Sarah knew she had been dismissed. She went downstairs and joined the three Armstrong girls in the parlor, where they sat huddled in misery.

Megan looked up at her with tearful eyes. "Is my pa going to die, Sarah?" she asked plaintively.

Sarah went to put an arm around her, with Tabitha. "Of course not, Meggie! He's going to be fine. Marcus says he was cut by a sword, but your ma has doctored him as good as any medical doctor, probably better. And Marcus says he just needs rest and nourishment to regain his strength. Marcus is a wise man," she assured them.

"Can we see him?" Tabitha asked.

"I think he's sleeping right now. I just carried the basin

of water up there for Hester, and Aunt Charity sent me back down here. But I'm sure you can see him later," she reassured them.

"What happened? Did they say?" Abigail asked.

Sarah shook her head. "Marcus said they were waylaid by bandits on the Jamestown Road." She didn't mention that he had as good as indicated that this was not really what happened.

"The Jamestown Road!" Tabitha repeated, as Aunt Charity had. "Ma will certainly never let us travel it again!"

"Oh, no!" Abigail wailed.

"Well, 'Gail, if there are bandits, I don't think we would want to be traveling on it anyway," Tabitha pointed out.

"But our lessons, Tabby!" Abigail wailed.

"Marcus told Aunt Charity we should be safe if we travel in daylight," Sarah said, "but he cautioned her to keep us at home at night."

Then he had quoted that mysterious verse that everybody keeps quoting. What could it mean, and why was her uncle involved in it?

Suddenly Sarah had the feeling that Uncle Ethan had not been hurt on a mission for the Patriots. It was something to do with that Bible verse. She just knew it was! But what? And how could she find out?

I look like a trussed turkey waiting to be baked!" Uncle Ethan commented, as he sat on the parlor sofa on his first evening downstairs. It had been nearly a week since his injury. "I saw your handiwork as I was shaving, dear," he continued. "I thought you were a better seamstress than that!"

"Well, Ethan, your head was gaping open like a sliced melon," Aunt Charity answered. "I had to sew it up! And I must say, sewing on silk or linen is much easier than trying to poke a needle through tough hide like yours! Be glad you were unconscious!"

"Be glad my hide is tough, my dear," he said, "or I might not be here at all. And be glad Marcus was with me, or I might have bled to death out there."

"Exactly where were you, Ethan?" Aunt Charity asked. "We don't really know what happened."

Sarah recognized her uncle's trapped look. "Marcus told

us you were waylaid by bandits on the Jamestown Road," she rescued him. "That's all we know, Uncle Ethan."

He threw her a grateful glance. "I didn't know what Marcus had told you," he said. "That's about it, I guess. I don't remember much after that, except Marcus putting me up on his horse in front of him and carrying me home."

"Ethan, I don't think these girls ought to travel that road, even if they have to give up their music and dancing lessons at Pleasantwood Plantation," Aunt Charity said. "Surely there's someone here in Williamsburg who could teach them!"

Abigail began to wring her hands. "Oh, Ma, please . . ."

Tabitha sat quietly, biting her lip.

Their father took in their obvious distress. "I believe they will be perfectly safe in the daylight, Charity," he said. "Bandits usually come out at night."

"'Men love darkness rather than light because their deeds are evil,'" Sarah quoted innocently.

Uncle Ethan gave her a long look.

"John 3:19," she said with a grin. "It's in the Bible."

He frowned. "Yes, I know, Sarah." He turned back to his wife. "Charity, I could send someone else along with Sam to guard the girls, if it would make you feel better. I can see that those lessons are very important, at least to some of them."

"Actually, it would make me feel better," Aunt Charity agreed, "if you insist on their going."

"Then that's settled. I know a young militiaman who would be happy to do me a favor—for a small fee," he said, rising slowly to his feet. "I think I've been up long enough for my first day," he added. "If you will steady me, my dear, I'll go upstairs to bed."

★ Chapter Seven ★

When they had left the room, Uncle Ethan leaning rather heavily on Aunt Charity's shoulder, Abigail danced around the room. "Pa has saved us!" she cried happily. "We'll be going back to Pleasantwood Plantation tomorrow afternoon! Oh, I can hardly wait!"

"For pity's sake, calm down, Abigail!" Tabitha ordered. "You'll make Ma change her mind, after all!"

"I wish she would," Megan said grumpily. "I don't want you all gallivanting all over the countryside, leaving me here at home alone."

"Don't be such a spoilsport, Meggie," Sarah said, catching the littie girl in a bear hug and swinging her off the floor.

"Put me down, Sarah!" she demanded, still pouting.

"Aw, come on, Meggie, let's take a walk before it gets completely dark. It won't be long, for the days are getting shorter and shorter."

"Let's go all the way down to the end of our street," Megan suggested, when they were standing outside the house, wrapped in their warm cloaks against the chill November wind.

"All right. I'll race you to Botetourt Street!" Sarah challenged.

They ran, laughing, to the corner where Botetourt joined Nicholson. Then Sarah reached for Megan's hand, and swinging it between them, continued on down toward the gaol, crossing to the other side of the street before they reached it, as Aunt Charity required.

"Do you 'member when they put your tutor in there," Megan asked suddenly, "and she was cold and hungry, and you and Ma and Tabitha sent her food and warm things?"

"Of course, I do, Meggie," Sarah answered, not wanting to remember. "You know, Jesus said we should clothe the poor, feed the hungry, and visit those in prison. It says so in the Bible."

"But she was a spy, Sarah! Are we s'posed to be good to spies? She tried to cause Pa trouble, maybe even get him killed."

"I know, Meggie, but the Bible also says to love our enemies, to do good to those who persecute us and despitefully use us." And Gabrielle certainly had despitefully used her, she thought.

She had read that instruction in her uncle's Bible, though. She tried to read the Bible every day, now that she was a Christian. She wished she had a Bible of her own so she wouldn't have to borrow Uncle Ethan's, though he had told her she could.

"The Bible says that when we do good to our enemies, we heap coals of fire on their heads."

"Well, Sarah, I don't think that's a very nice thing to do!" Megan said indignantly. "That's worse than . . . than slapping them on the other cheek, like Ma says."

"No, Meggie, your ma says we should turn the other cheek when someone slaps us. That's in the Bible, too," she added.

"Look, Sarah, that's her house, isn't it? That brown one down there, with the pretty blue door. I don't think anybody lives there now. Hester says the house is cursed."

"That's ridiculous, Meggie," Sarah began, noting that they had reached the corner of Waller Street before she knew it. She hadn't intended to come this far.

"Well, your tutor's house is empty, Sarah. See? The milliner's sign still hangs there. Hester says no one wants to live in the house of a British spy."

"The house had nothing to do with it. And, anyway, the

house never belonged to . . ."

She stopped. Was that a light in Gabrielle's house? If no one lived there, why would there be a light? She didn't see it now, though. Maybe she had imagined it.

"Somebody's in there, Sarah!" Megan said. "I saw a light."

"Come on, Meggie, let's go home," she urged.

"What's the matter, Sarah? Are you afraid? Who do you think it could be?"

"I don't know, Meggie, but it's getting dark out here, and Aunt Charity will have a fit if we are out after dark, especially after Uncle Ethan's encounter with those bandits." Or whatever he had encountered, she thought.

"I know!" the little girl said. "It's a ghost! The ghost of your tutor, Sarah."

"Meggie, don't be silly!" Sarah scolded. "Gabrielle isn't dead. It can't be her ghost. Anyway, there's no such thing as ghosts." *Except the ghosts of memory that always will haunt me any time I see this house or think of Gabrielle,* she thought.

"Is too," Megan argued. "Hester says there's ghosts all over Williamsburg. There's ghostly footsteps at Wythe House, and some at the President's House at the college, and there's the spirit of that dead Indian boy who still runs from Brafferton Hall across the college grounds some nights. There's even one or two ghosts at Randolph House right on our street! Ask Hester. She'll tell you."

"I don't doubt that she would," Sarah said sarcastically. "Meggie, Hester has no business filling a little girl's mind with such rubbish. I think you're spending too much time with her." Sarah caught her breath. There was the light again, flickering in the windows of the little brown house.

"Well, I wouldn't have to if you and Tabby and 'Gail would stay at home!" Megan retorted. "Sarah, are you listening? What are you looking at? Oh!" she gasped, clutching Sarah's hand.

Could Hester be right? Sarah wondered. Was there a ghost in Gabrielle's house? Nonsense! she scolded herself. If there were a light in the house, someone was in there, and it was no ghost. But who could it be? Should she go down there, knock on the door, and see what happened?

The cold wind whispered through the dry oak leaves and murmured in the cedars. The house sat deep in the shadows cast by the pale November moon. Sarah shivered.

"You're not going down there, are you, Sarah?" Megan's voice trembled. "Ghosts sometimes get violet, you know."

"Violet? Oh, Meggie, you mean violent."

"Whatever," the little girl muttered. "Anyway, sometimes they are angry and hurt people."

"Is that another one of Hester's stories?" Sarah asked

scornfully. "Meggie, how many times do I have to tell you there is no such thing as a ghost? Come on, I'll prove it to you."

She took the little girl by the hand and half-dragged her down the street until they stood directly across from Gabrielle's house.

She could see no light now, but determined to prove her point, she marched Meggie resolutely across the street and onto the stoop before the bright blue door. She reached out, hesitated a moment, then knocked firmly.

The wind moaned around the corners of the building and caught in their cloaks. Sarah shivered and drew hers closer about her. She saw Meggie do the same.

"Let's go home, Sarah!" the little girl whispered. "I'm cold and I'm scared!"

"So am I, Meggie, but we've come this far, and we're going to see this through." She knocked again, louder this time.

"Did you hear that, Sarah?" Megan whispered. Sarah could feel the little girl's fear through her trembling hand.

"What, Meggie? What did you hear?"

"I don't know. Something is in there. Moving around. Trying to keep quiet," she whispered.

"Is anybody there?" Sarah called. She knocked again. After some time had passed with no response, she turned away. "All right, Meggie, we'll go home," she said.

"Thank you!" Megan breathed. This time it was the little girl who pulled Sarah by the hand up the street.

When they reached the Armstrong gate, Sarah stopped her. "Megan, don't say anything to anybody about where we've been," she warned. "Aunt Charity has enough on her mind right now."

"But, Sarah, we may have seen a ghost! I have to tell Hester, and Tabby and 'Gail!"

"No, you don't," Sarah ordered. "If you do, I will never go anywhere with you again. But if you can keep our secret, I will share more with you."

The little girl thought about that for a moment. "All right, Sarah," she agreed hesitantly, "I won't say anything right now. But one of these days I'll just bust wide open and that big old secret will come pouring out. I won't be able to stop it."

Sarah laughed. "All right, Meggie. I understand. Just please don't say anything right now. Promise? Give me some time to find out what's going on down there."

"I promise," Meggie said solemnly. "But I know what's going on. A ghost has moved into the little brown house."

Sarah sighed. "Meggie, what will I ever do with you?" she asked. "I just can't convince you of anything!"

"You convinced me to quit saying 'tootler' for 'tutor,' " Megan said seriously. Then she laughed. "I can't believe I said such a dumb thing, and just last year!"

"Well, I'll tell you what, Miss Grown-Up Megan Armstrong," Sarah said, opening the gate and leading the little girl to the front door, "Let's go inside, and I'll make us some hot chocolate to chase away the chill of that November wind."

"And to chase away the chill of the ghost?" Meggie asked with a grin.

Sarah threw up her hands in surrender. "And the ghost," she agreed, laughing.

Friday dawned with a drizzling rain falling. By afternoon, the gray skies showed no sign of lightening, and the rain had not let up. Reluctantly, Aunt Charity gave in to Abigail and Tabitha's persuasions to let them go to Pleasantwood Plantation for their music and dancing lessons.

"Make sure they are home well before dark," she cautioned Sam and the young militiaman who sat beside him on the driver's seat outside the covered part of the carriage.

"Did you notice who is riding up there with Sam?" Tabitha asked excitedly, when they were rolling down the road, secure from the rain inside the cozy carriage.

Sarah, riding backward because her cousins both had insisted that riding backward made them ill, had to admit she hadn't noticed. But Sam and the soldier were so bundled up in rain gear that she barely had been able to recognize Sam.

"It's Seth! Seth Coler!" Tabitha said. "If only Pa knew

who he has sent to guard me!"

"Kind of like sending the fox to guard the chicken coop?" Abigail said. "Or it would be, if Seth knew you were alive!"

Tabitha threw her sister a hurt look. "He knows I'm alive," she said hesitantly. "He looks at me all the time in church."

"Oh, pooh, Tabby!" Abigail retorted. "The militiamen look at all the girls. It's what they do for entertainment during those long, dry sermons. I still say Seth Coler doesn't know you're alive!"

"Never you mind, Miss Abigail Armstrong," Tabitha said haughtily. "If he isn't already aware of my existence, which he is, I guarantee he will know I am alive before this day is over!"

Oh, no! Sarah thought. *'Gail has pushed our gentle tabby cat too far. What will she do to make Seth notice her?* Sarah hoped that whatever it was, it wouldn't embarrass them all too much.

When they stopped before the plantation house, Seth helped the girls from the carriage, and Tabitha said sweetly, "I hate to see you riding out there in the rain, Lieutenant. Sam has to, of course, to drive, but there's no reason for you to be miserable, too. On the way home, why don't you join us in the carriage?"

"Why . . . ah . . . thank you, ma'am!" he stammered, touching the brim of his dripping hat with his fingers. "If you are sure it will be all right with Colonel Armstrong."

"Of course, it will!" Tabitha insisted. "I'm sure our pa would be happy to know that we have such good protection right inside our carriage."

I'm not! Sarah thought, as they made their way up to the

back doors and the carriage drove on around the semicircle to the stables. If Uncle Ethan had wanted his guard stationed inside the carriage, Sarah was sure he would have made that clear before they left home.

Oh, well, she decided, as the big doors swung open, *I don't have any dog in that fight!* And she followed her cousins inside and up the stairs to the music room.

Señor Alfredo was waiting for them. "Good afternoon, señoritas!" he said, bending over their hands with a kiss for each. "I have such exciting things planned for us today!"

Abigail acts as stupid over Señor Alfredo as Tabitha does over Seth Coler, Sarah thought, watching her cousin simper and smirk at the dancing master. It was incomprehensible to Sarah what her cousins saw in either of the men. But, as Pa always said, "If everybody had the same taste, somebody would go hungry."

Today, Señor Alfredo assigned Abigail to play the harpsichord, while he danced first with Tabitha, then with Sarah, taking all patience to instruct her in the minuet. Then he asked Tabitha to play while he danced with Abigail. The dancing improved greatly, though the music did not. He and Abigail hardly seemed to notice, however, as they glided as one across the floor. Abigail's face wore that absurd besotted expression, but her dancing was superb.

Soon bored with watching, Sarah went in search of a drink. Surely it would be all right if she asked one of the kitchen maids for a glass of water. The dancing had made her thirsty.

She wandered down the hallway, using her errand as an excuse to explore a little.

On the back side of the house, across from the music room, there was a small parlor, a study, and an elaborate bedroom suite with a dressing room and bath. On the other side of the hall, the music room left space only for a bedroom, tucked in the corner near the elusive staircase that she felt sure must descend to the kitchens.

The bedroom door stood open, and Sarah saw a tall bedstead covered with a cream-colored spread, a dresser holding masculine toilet accessories, a small table with books and papers on it, and a wingback chair before the fireplace. Near the chair, a music stand held papers bearing musical notes. A silver flute lay on the chair.

This had to be Señor Alfredo's room, she reasoned, and before she knew it, Sarah was inside, her curiosity getting the better of her judgment. Uncle Ethan had warned her about that just the other night, she remembered. But as she was already in the room, she decided she might as well look around.

She went to the dresser and fingered the elaborate silver carvings on the tortoiseshell brush and comb she found there. The initials "A.A." were entwined amid the design.

Then she examined the books on the table that was obviously used as a desk, but they were all Spanish titles and she could not read them. It was the same with the papers on the desk and the music on the stand.

She would not pry into closed drawers, Sarah told herself, but the door of the armoire stood open. Inside, she could see the fashionable tight black trousers of the day hanging beside velvet and brocade waistcoats. One short jacket bore an elaborate embroidered scene of bulls and matadors.

Suddenly, Sarah heard footsteps. Her heart began to pound as she looked around for somewhere to hide. She couldn't be caught here, in such flagrant disregard for the music and dancing master's privacy! Quickly, she crossed the room and hid behind the open door.

The footsteps stopped, then began again. But they did not pass in the hallway outside. Suddenly, Megan's stories of ghostly footsteps came back to her. Did Pleasantwood Plantation have a ghost of its own? She felt the hairs rise on the back of her neck. Had she antagonized some restless spirit by being here uninvited?

Finally, gathering her courage, she moved to where she could see into the hallway. There was no one there, yet the footsteps continued. Then she realized that they were coming from overhead! There must be an attic. Perhaps some of the servants lived there, as they did in many of Williamsburg's finer homes, she reasoned with relief. Someone must be up there restlessly pacing the floor.

Sarah fled down the hallway and down the narrow back stairs, where a small landing opened into a large kitchen. A black woman stirring something in a kettle over the fire in the fireplace turned to look at her in surprise as she came through the swinging door.

"I . . . I'm here taking music and dancing lessons with Señor Alfredo," she explained. "May I have a drink of water? Dancing is hard work!" She laughed nervously.

The woman went to the sink, pumped a glass of water, and handed it to her without comment. Sarah gulped the cold water thirstily and held out the glass for more. When she had finished about half of the second glass, she handed it back to the woman, who poured it into a drain right there in the sink.

How Hester would love a drain that carried water right out of the kitchen without having to tote it in a bucket! She'd have to tell Aunt Charity and Uncle Ethan about it.

Then Sarah heard carriage wheels outside. Looking out

the tall windows to her right, she saw the Armstrong carriage pull up at the back doors.

"Thank you so much!" she said to the woman, who had yet to make a sound. "How do I get to the driveway where our carriage is waiting?"

Silently, the woman showed her through the kitchen area and dining rooms to the front hallway, where the butler let her out.

Abigail and Tabitha already were in the carriage when Seth helped her in and climbed in after her, shutting the door behind him.

"Are you sure Colonel Armstrong won't mind me riding inside with you ladies?" Seth asked Tabitha.

"Oh, no!" her cousin answered quickly, motioning Sarah into the seat beside Abigail and moving over to ride backward beside the soldier on the seat facing them. Sarah smiled, remembering her cousin's earlier claims to illness when forced to ride backward.

★ Chapter Eight ★

"Has your wound healed, Lieutenant?" Tabitha inquired. "I hear you are a real war hero." She smiled sweetly and reached out to touch him on the arm.

I think I'm going to be sick, Sarah thought, *and it has nothing to do with riding positions.* She glanced at Abigail, but she was either unusually absorbed in the wet scenery outside the carriage, or wrapped in dreams of her own. Tabitha's obvious flirting was something Sarah might have expected from the sly Abigail, but she had never dreamed Tabitha had it in her! Seth was eating it up, though.

Tuning out their light patter, Sarah turned her thoughts to more interesting matters, such as what the men meant when they whispered the mysterious John 3:19, and who might be living in Gabrielle's house.

Suddenly, Sarah wondered if Seth might have the answer to either of those questions.

"Lieutenant?" she began.

"Yes, ma'am?" he answered, his eyes never leaving Tabitha's face, his expression as goofy as hers.

"Do you know who is living in the house of the milliner Gabrielle Gordon?" Sarah asked.

He turned to look at her then, and Sarah sensed that he was uncomfortable with her question. "Why, I believe the house is empty, ma'am," he said, dropping his gaze to his hands folded in his lap. Then he looked up at her again. "Why? Have you seen someone there?"

"No, it's just that my little cousin, Megan, and I took a walk down that way last night and thought we saw a light inside the house. Meggie was convinced it was a ghost." She laughed.

"I'm sure the place is empty," he repeated seriously, looking away from her. "No one wants to live there now."

"Are you familiar with John 3:19?" Sarah asked, curious to see his reaction to the verse she had heard whispered by her uncle and others involved in . . . whatever they were involved in.

The young lieutenant wouldn't look at her. "I believe it's a Bible verse, ma'am," he answered finally.

"Sarah!" Tabitha scolded. "Such questions! I'm sure the lieutenant cares nothing for Megan's ghosts or your cryptic references to the Bible." She smiled sweetly at Seth, and he looked back at her adoringly.

Oh, bother! Sarah thought, giving up and joining Abigail in her scrutiny of the countryside. "It's a lovely day for a drive, isn't it, 'Gail?" she said sarcastically.

Abigail turned to look at her, but Sarah could see that her thoughts were somewhere else, back at Pleasantwood Plantation with Señor Alfredo, she supposed.

Sarah sighed. She had more important things to think about than making calf's eyes over some man. She was going to find the answers to her questions if it killed her! And, like Uncle Ethan's cat that was done in by curiosity, it might, she thought. But she was going to find out who was in Gabrielle's house, and why. And she was going to discover what that elusive Bible verse meant to the men of Williamsburg, or die trying!

Marcus was the key, she decided. She doubted if he knew anything about the little brown house, unless he had picked up some gossip somewhere, but he surely knew what was going on with that Bible verse! And, when they got home, she vowed, he was going to tell her!

The drizzle had turned into a steady downpour by the time they reached the Armstrong house, and the dark gray sky had shut down over Williamsburg like a lid on a kettle. It would be dark in minutes.

Sarah knew it would be foolish to venture over to the palace gardens on such a night. Anyway, Marcus would most likely be at home with Dulcie and Sam, when the boy finished unhitching the carriage and stabling the horses. She wanted to talk to Marcus alone.

The next morning, the rain had stopped, but a chill wind had taken its place. The sun apparently had no intention of getting involved in such a day.

Aunt Charity was busy in the kitchen with Hester, since Saturday was her baking day, when the week's supply of breads and cakes for the Armstrong household was prepared.

Abigail had been assigned the task of transferring hot coals from the fireplace to the firebox of the oven with a small shovel. Tabitha was washing and drying pans and bowls for further use as fast as they were empty. Sarah and Megan were seated on the hearth, cracking walnuts, extracting the succulent kernels from the shells, and chopping them for some of the cakes.

"How are the dancing lessons coming along, girls?" Aunt Charity asked, as she kneaded bread dough on a square board on the worktable in the center of the room. "Are you ready to impress everyone at the Governor's Ball?"

Sarah laughed. "I'll impress them, all right, Aunt Charity, with my clumsiness!"

"Oh, Sarah, you've made great progress with the minuet, and your curtsy is second only to mine," Abigail said generously.

"And you, Tabitha?" Aunt Charity asked. "Are you ready for the ball?"

When Tabitha didn't answer, Sarah turned to see her cousin standing with her hands in a pan of steaming, soapy water, lost in her dreams.

"Tabitha?" her mother repeated.

Tabitha jumped and knocked a dish off the drainboard into the pan. "I'm sorry, Ma," she apologized. "I guess I wasn't listening. What did you say?"

Aunt Charity studied her oldest daughter for a moment. "I asked if you were ready for the ball," she repeated finally.

"Oh, well, I'm . . . working on it," Tabitha stammered, her face turning red for no apparent reason.

"Tabitha, what on earth is wrong with you?" Aunt Charity asked. "You've been off in some other world all day. Are you ill?"

"I think she's just sick with love, Ma," Abigail said, laughing, "and what she's working on is getting the wonderful Seth Coler to dance with her at the ball."

"Seth Coler?" Aunt Charity said, frowning. "Isn't that the young militiaman your father has asked to escort you to Pleasantwood Plantation?"

Tabitha threw Abigail a look of anger, mingled with despair. "Yes, Ma, it is," she answered truthfully.

Aunt Charity gave Tabitha a long, hard look, then went back to kneading her bread dough. "Your dresses are nearly ready," she said. "I think we will have a fitting this afternoon, after we've cleared away this mess."

Sarah had to admit that Aunt Charity, cold as she seemed at times, had put a lot of care and effort into the dresses, hers as well as the other girls'. When she had finished pinning and tucking the new dresses to a perfect fit, Aunt Charity let the girls admire themselves in the full-length mirror in her room.

Abigail's dress was a powder blue, exactly the color of her eyes, with a full, sweeping skirt that, as she twirled around the floor, gave an added grace to her movements. It was obvious how she felt about herself in it, Sarah thought, but her pride was justified, for she looked lovely.

Tabitha's gown was a deep red that lent color to her fair cheeks and put a glow in her eyes. Or maybe the glow was from some other source, Sarah thought with amusement. She pitied anybody as besotted with love as Tabitha apparently was.

Sarah's dress was a brilliant emerald green silk that deepened her green eyes and set off the reddish highlights of her dark hair. "If I were ever going to be pretty," she told herself, as she preened this way and that in front of the mirror, "it would be in this dress." But she still had freckles sprinkled across her nose, she noted honestly, and what would she ever do with her poker-straight hair? She supposed she would have to sleep on curlers the night before the ball.

"You look beautiful, Sarah," Megan said from behind her. "I'll never look like you no matter how many ruffles and ribbons Ma sews on my dress!"

"Your new dress is lovely, Meggie, and you look lovely in it," Sarah said, looking her over carefully. "That yellow looks just like sunlight and sets your dark eyes to dancing. Why, you'll be the prettiest girl at the ball, Miss Megan Armstrong!"

"I love you, Sarah," the little girl said, throwing both arms around her.

"I love you, too, Meggie," Sarah responded, gently removing the small arms before they could crease the green silk.

"Do you think I will have a good time at the ball?" Megan asked then. "I've never been to a ball before."

"Oh, yes, Meggie, I know you will. There's to be a room especially devoted to children's entertainment, and there will be so many tempting treats to sample that we will all come away ten pounds heavier than when we went!"

Megan giggled. "Will there be fried chicken? It's my fav'rite, you know."

"I don't know about that," Sarah answered, laughing. "You know, Meggie, I've never been to a ball, either. We will share our first ball, and I'm sure we will find plenty of foods there to tickle our fancies."

Aunt Charity clapped her hands. "Girls, enough preening!" she said. "Get out of those dresses before you ruin them and have nothing to wear to the ball. It's only three weeks away. There's no time to make more!"

Sarah took off her dress and reluctantly handed it to her

aunt. The other girls apparently felt the same way about surrendering their new finery.

"Let's go downstairs and pop some popcorn!" Abigail suggested. "The new crop should be dry enough to pop by now."

Sarah glanced out the window, then at the clock on Aunt Charity's mantel. Though the sun never had decided to show its face, it was only four in the afternoon. And it was the first chance she had had to visit Marcus.

"You all go ahead," she said. "I have an errand to do, then I will join you."

"Where are you going, Sarah?" Megan asked. "Can I go with you?"

"Not this time, Meggie," she said. "You stay here and help shell the popcorn. I'll be back in three shakes of a dead sheep's tail."

"Sarah Moore, you know a dead sheep can't shake its tail!" Megan said indignantly. "You told me that the other day, and it took me the longest time to figure it out, but it just means you can stay away as long as you want to, because that tail is never going to shake!"

Sarah laughed and tousled the little girl's hair. "You're just too smart for me, Meggie," she sighed. "I can't put anything over on you, can I? But I really won't be gone long," she promised. "Save me some popcorn!"

Taking her cloak from the front closet, Sarah left the house and hurried down Nicholson Street to North England, and then across to the palace and its gardens, hoping Marcus would be there.

She went through the gates and followed the graveled paths to keep out of yesterday's mud. Finally, she located Marcus, raking leaves down in the lower gardens.

"I didn't know if you'd be here on a day like today," she said.

"Well, missy, the flower beds don't know what color the sky is, and they need mulching for the winter," he answered. "What are you doing out on such a day?"

"Well, Marcus, I've been wanting to talk to you and–"

"Miss Sarah, if it's about your uncle and his mishap the other night, I can't tell you any more than I already told you," he interrupted, stopping his work to look her directly in the eyes.

She shook her head. "That's not it, exactly. I want to know what John 3:19 means and why everybody goes around quoting it."

He went back to his raking. "Miss Sarah, since that day when you gave me that cup of cold apple juice when I was sweltering in those stocks, ole Marcus has never denied you anything you asked him, except that time you asked me to take you off to Norfolk without telling your uncle."

"I don't hold that against you, Marcus," she interrupted. "You helped me, after all, and I got to see Gabrielle."

"But, honey, you're asking for something now that's not mine to give. The code, John 3:19, stands for something that involves a lot of people, and if its secrets fell into the wrong hands, some of them could get hurt, maybe even killed."

"It's what Uncle Ethan was involved in the night he was hurt, isn't it?" she asked.

He nodded. "Yes, Miss Sarah, it is, and the less you know about it, the better for you and everybody else."

"But, Marcus, I swear I wouldn't tell anybody! Not even Tabitha and Abigail."

"It's not nice to swear, honey. The Bible says—"

"I promise, then. It was just an expression," she said

GRACE CHRISTIAN
SCHOOL LIBRARY

impatiently. "I know what the Bible says. I read it every day. And I've read John 3:19. I understand that men love darkness rather than light when they want to do evil deeds under its cover. But I don't know what men, and I don't know what deeds. Please tell me, Marcus! Maybe I can help."

"Miss Sarah, you wouldn't have a bit more business being involved in this than . . . than those beautiful swans over there have in being involved with a . . . a wildcat!"

A wildcat, she thought. That was what Gabrielle had called her. "Marcus, I've fought Indians. I've survived blizzards. I've lived surrounded by wild animals. I'm not a . . . a pampered flower to be protected from the weather."

"Honey, this thing involves a darker darkness and a greater evil than you can imagine. And your uncle and Marcus and many others are trying to bring light into that darkness. That's all I can tell you. Now, if you want to visit a while, let's talk about something else."

She sat down heavily on a bench at the end of one of the

flower beds. "Are you involved with the Governor's Ball?" she asked, a hint of sarcasm creeping into her voice. "Can you talk about that?"

"I sure can, missy. In fact, my Dulcie has been asked to sing at the ball. Can you imagine that? A black woman! But there's nobody in Virginia, black or white, with a voice like Dulcie's."

"I know," Sarah said. "I've heard her. And you're right, she does sing like a wild canary, or maybe an angel."

He smiled. "That's what Governor Henry said, an angel. I got her a job helping in the kitchen here at the palace, and Dulcie sometimes just can't help singing as she goes about her chores. Anyway, the governor heard her and asked her to sing at the ball. Of course, Dulcie's shy, but the governor said she could sing from behind a screen, where nobody would be staring at her. She has agreed to do it."

"Oh, Marcus, what an honor! And she is so deserving of it!"

He nodded. "Yes, she is," he said. "She truly is."

Sarah left the gardens more excited about the ball than she had been even when she had tried on the green silk dress earlier that afternoon. Dulcie's singing would be something to look forward to, even if her own dancing left something to be desired, she thought as she hurried along Nicholson Street.

It was little darker than it had been all afternoon, but she could see lights glowing from most of the houses.

Suddenly, she wondered if there would be a light on in the little brown house, and she passed up the Armstrong gate and walked on toward Waller Street.

Was somebody living in Gabrielle's house, maybe some vagrant who wanted a place to stay without paying a lease? Or maybe it was a Tory who was loyal to the king of England and felt the need to hide from the Patriot army. Whoever it was, Sarah didn't believe it was a ghost.

She turned the corner onto Waller Street. Sarah didn't believe in Meggie's and Hester's ghosts, though she had almost believed in them over at Pleasantwood Plantation that afternoon.

She walked up and down in front of the little brown house, but there was no light showing in its windows. She half-turned to go back when she noticed something. The milliner's sign was gone! She knew it had been there on Thursday. Today it was gone, only the pole remaining to show where it had swung.

Sarah crossed the street, opened the wooden gate, and went slowly up the brick walk to the front stoop. She knocked loudly on the door. If someone were staying here, she wanted to know who it was. Surely she would be in no danger, out in plain sight of all of Waller Street, with patrons coming and going from Christiana Campbell's busy tavern next door!

It was getting colder as she waited to see if anyone would answer her knock. There was more than a hint of frost in the November wind that whispered through the oak leaves still clinging to their branches and swept the leaves of the less determined maples along the yards and streets.

Sarah knocked again. There was no answer, and she could hear no movement inside, as Meggie had insisted she had heard the other night.

She left the stoop and walked around the house. At the back, she tried to peer through a window and found it covered with some dark material. As she continued around the house, she found that all the windows were similarly covered.

Sarah pictured in her mind Gabrielle's dainty curtains. There had been no dark drapes in the cheerful little house. These had been added, possibly since Thursday night, when she and Megan had seen the light inside the house. Someone was staying here, she decided, and he didn't want anyone to know it!

What should she do? Uncle Ethan really wasn't able to do anything about it right now. Anyway, he and Marcus, the two men she had thought she could trust with her life, both had refused to trust her with the meaning of that Bible verse. If they knew anything about this house, they likely wouldn't share it with her.

If only there were some way she could get inside the house! But how? If she knew who the owner was, she could pretend to want to rent it and ask to see inside. But she was only thirteen years old. He wouldn't believe her.

Tabitha! she thought. Tabitha was fifteen. Lots of girls got married at that age. Sarah could say Tabitha was looking for a cottage to live in after her wedding. But everybody in Williamsburg knew everybody else. Whoever owned the little house surely would know Aunt Charity and Uncle Ethan. They would ask questions about the coming wedding, and her aunt and uncle would find out.

Anyway, she thought, as she walked around the house again, she shouldn't be plotting to tell lies. She was a Christian, and that certainly wasn't Christian behavior.

Suddenly, the back door opened and a small black boy ran out. He was a little smaller than her brother Jamie, she reckoned, probably about three years old, but he had that same little-boy sweetness about him, from his tight curly hair to his bare black feet. She smiled at him, and he stuck his thumb in his mouth, watching her with wide dark eyes.

A black woman ran out the door, calling to the boy in a loud whisper, flapping her hands at him in a gesture that obviously meant, "Come here!" When she saw Sarah standing there, the woman froze in her tracks. Sarah never had seen such terror on anyone's face! The woman ran to the boy, scooped him up in her arms, ran back inside the house, and slammed the door. Sarah heard the bolt slide into place.

For a moment, Sarah stood there, as frozen as the woman had been. People *were* living in Gabrielle's house! And it was plain that they didn't want anyone to know it. The woman had spoken some strange tongue that Sarah had never heard before. Who were these people? And why were they hiding in the little brown house?

Maybe they were escaped slaves, Sarah thought, as she

made her way back around the house and onto the street. She heard of such things now and then. But how had they gotten into Gabrielle's house? There were no signs of forced entry. Someone with a key must have unlocked the door for them.

All the way back to the Armstrong house, Sarah tried to find answers to her questions, but there were none. Maybe she should just go in and talk with her uncle about all this. Surely he would know what to do.

Sarah remembered the little boy and how he had reminded her of her little brother, Jamie, except that his skin was so much darker. Then she remembered the terror on the woman's face. She didn't want to hurt them. She didn't even want to scare them. But her uncle was a kind and understanding man. She was sure he would do what was best for everyone concerned.

Then the memory of Uncle Ethan paying the auctioneer for the three slaves came into her mind. There hadn't been a chance to question him about it. Did he talk one way about slavery and live another? He hadn't brought them home to serve his family. They hadn't been taken to the Governor's Palace. Why had he bought them, and what had happened to them?

Marcus had been involved. Surely he would do nothing to hurt his own people! What on earth was going on here?

Sarah found her uncle in his study, sitting behind the big desk, working on some papers.

"How are you feeling, Uncle Ethan?" she asked.

"Much better, thank you, Sarah." Then he looked up at her quizzically. "Why? Are you going to tell me something I don't want to hear? What have you been up to now, young lady?" He grinned, but she knew his concern was genuine.

★ Chapter Ten ★

"I haven't been up to anything, Uncle Ethan," she answered, "but I have discovered something I think you should know." And she told him about the little brown house, beginning with the night she and Megan had seen the light, and ending with her encounter with the black woman and the little boy a few minutes ago.

Her uncle sighed deeply. "Sarah, Sarah," he said wearily, "why can't you be content to embroider pillowcases, like Tabitha, or to play the harpsichord, like Abigail? Why must you always be nosing into things that don't concern you, that could even be dangerous for you to know?"

She said nothing, and her uncle leaned toward her across the desk and folded his hands together. "All right, Sarah," he said, "shut the door. I am going to share something with you that you cannot share with another living soul—not your cousins, not your friends, not even your Aunt Charity."

Sarah shut the door and came back to sit in the chair in front of the desk, anticipation tingling her spine.

"I believe I can trust you not to repeat what I am going to tell you, and it may be easier than trying to keep secrets from you. You are so persistent!" he said. "But let me warn you again, Sarah. The lives of Marcus, myself, and many others could be in grave danger if you so much as let one word slip!"

Still, she said nothing. She didn't know what to say. She just waited, holding her breath for fear he would not continue.

"I am involved in a venture to end the importation of slaves to Virginia, or at least to the Williamsburg area," he said. "As we have discussed before, a law has been passed that forbids anyone to bring slaves into Virginia from Africa or the West Indies, or even from other states, except in cases in which someone relocates here and brings his own slaves with him."

Sarah nodded. He had told her about the law before. The slaves here in the capital city were well-educated and highly trained, and the people of Williamsburg objected to the bringing in of foreign slaves who were unskilled and spoke no English. If they could not be used for menial chores on the plantations, they often were turned loose to roam the countryside.

"So people are bringing slaves in from other places in spite of the law?" she asked.

"Yes, and not only that," he continued, "these smugglers pack the poor people into the holds of ships like sardines, to lie in their own filth for weeks on the journey over here, throwing them just enough food to keep them alive to sell once they get here, throwing them overboard when they die. They care nothing for human misery. In fact, they claim the black people aren't human, which they think excuses their actions."

"Won't God punish them for that?"

"I believe He will, Sarah, someday. But these smugglers believe in no god except the gold they can make."

"Why don't you just arrest them, Uncle Ethan?" she asked. "Surely the law is on your side! Why must you and Marcus sneak around after dark, risking your own lives to do . . . whatever you do?"

"We intercept the shipments of slaves as they are unloaded on the James, and other places, and see that the slaves are fed, cared for, and then shipped back to Africa or the islands. They are eager to go, since most of them have been taken by force from their homes, sold into captivity by their enemies there."

★ Chapter Ten ★

"The black people I saw in Gabrielle's house," she said, "do you know about them?"

He nodded. "We have been using the house as a hiding place until we can ship them out. I have rented it from the owner. He thinks I want it for storage, which I suppose I do." He chuckled. "We forgot about the milliner's sign inviting visitors until yesterday, when we took it down."

"And you have placed dark drapes over the windows to hide any light that might show from the house."

He nodded again. "We have asked them not to use light except for the fireplaces, which they need for warmth and for cooking. But they don't always understand. They speak no English. Sam has been a big help with the ones from the islands, since his mother taught him the island language as a child."

"Are there smuggled slaves hidden at Pleasantwood Plantation, Uncle Ethan?" she asked. "I thought I heard footsteps in the attic over there, when most of the slaves should have been at work."

He shook his head. "Sarah, I'm glad you are on our side!" But he didn't answer her question about Pleasantwood.

"Virginians are allowed to raise their own slaves on their own property, or to trade among themselves," he continued. "There still will be auctions of slaves to settle estates or to pay off debts, though most slaves in Williamsburg are sold through modest newspaper ads or by word of mouth. I, for one, believe all slavery should be abolished, that if we want the service of other human beings, we should pay for it, as we do for Hester's help. But many people hold the opposite view."

"Uncle Ethan, I saw you buy three slaves at the auction the other day," Sarah said. "I know you to be a man of your word. If you don't believe in slavery, why did you buy them and what did you do with them?"

He smiled at her. "I suppose you saw Governor Henry, Thomas Jefferson, and George Wythe with me?" She nodded. "We pooled our money to buy those slaves because we had heard a cruel man was prepared to buy them. He especially had his eye on the young girl. We have given them free papers and sent them out of Virginia."

"Wouldn't it be easier just to buy the smuggled slaves and set them free?"

He laughed. "You must think that cedar tree out back grows money instead of cedar berries, Sarah! A strong black male who could have been bought for 100 pounds before the war now brings 1,000 pounds. It would take more money than the four of us have together to buy so many at such a price, and most of us have invested very heavily in the needs of this war. Anyway, these slave smugglers don't deserve to make a profit from the human misery they create."

"Uncle Ethan, why does God allow such evil to exist?" Sarah asked. "Why does He tolerate such things as slavery, especially when slave owners are cruel?"

"Sarah, I don't know. God works in mysterious ways sometimes, and I admit I don't always understand them."

"Do you believe Burwick will have to pay for what he did to Dulcie and Sam?" she persisted. "Someday, I mean, when he stands before the Judgment Seat of God?"

He studied her seriously for a moment. "Yes, Sarah, I do, but there are those who would hasten his punishment!"

He arose from his chair and stretched. "Now, young lady, I have been very generous, I think, with answers to your questions, but the well is exhausted. There are no more answers."

★ Chapter Ten ★

"But I have one more question, Uncle Ethan," she said. "What does John 3:19 mean? I have figured out it must be a code, and it must relate to this fighting against the slave trade, but—"

"There will be no more answers," he repeated firmly.

"Yes, sir. Thank you, sir," she said, and left the study.

Sarah walked down Waller Street every evening the next week but one, when it was pouring down rain, but there was no further sign of life at the little brown house.

On Thursday evening, Uncle Ethan went out after supper. Sarah was sure he had gone on another mission related to the slave smugglers. She wondered if her Aunt Charity had any idea what her husband was doing out there on this cold, dark November night, but Sarah said nothing to her or to her cousins.

They all sat in the parlor, Abigail looking at a book of fashions, Tabitha sketching a new embroidery design, and Sarah reading a story to Megan. Aunt Charity made a pretense of putting finishing touches on the ball gowns, but Sarah saw her eyes stray to the clock every few minutes.

She was worried about Uncle Ethan, too, remembering how he had come home last time, bleeding and nearly unconscious. There wasn't anything either she or Aunt

★ Chapter Eleven ★

Charity could do, though, but pray that he and the others with him would come home safely when their work was done.

When they finally went to bed, Sarah lay awake in the soft featherbed beside Megan, listening to her aunt pacing the floor of her bedroom. Out back, the cedar tree whispered and moaned in the wind. She shivered. Was it trying to tell them something—something cold and frightening?

She must have dozed then, for she was awakened by the clock in the downstairs hallway striking midnight. Soon after that, she heard the door open and footsteps wearily mounting the stairs. She heard her uncle talking softly with her aunt, then the house grew quiet, except for the continued murmuring of the cedar tree. Now, though, the sound was comforting, and Sarah drifted into a dreamless sleep.

The next afternoon, they traveled to Pleasantwood Plantation for their session with Señor Alfredo. Some older militiaman that Sarah had never seen before had taken Seth's place on the driver's seat beside Sam.

"Pa must have found out about your and Seth's making eyes at each other and asked for someone else to guard us," Abigail said.

"It's your fault, Abigail!" Tabitha snapped, her disappointment apparent in her bad temper. "You told Ma!"

"Tabitha Armstrong," Abigail said indignantly, "I can't believe you would think such a thing! I didn't say a word about his riding inside with us last week."

"Well, I'm sure Sarah didn't tell him, and Megan didn't know, so if Pa found out, it had to come from you."

"It most certainly did not!" Abigail insisted. "So I suppose your beloved just had more important business elsewhere today."

★ **Whispers in Williamsburg** ★

Suddenly Sarah remembered Uncle Ethan's mysterious errand the night before. Had Seth gone with him and been the one injured this time? She truly hoped not. He already had been wounded in the war, and had just gotten his arm out of the sling a few weeks ago.

Señor Alfredo greeted them in the music room. "Ah, señoritas, we must work very hard today, for the ball is not far off, no?"

He began the lesson with Tabitha, but it was obvious that her mind wasn't on her dancing. Finally, he stopped.

"Come, come, Señorita Tabitha," he scolded gently, "you dance with all the grace of a wooden doll today! Are you ill?"

Tabitha shook her head, looking as if she was about to burst into tears.

"It is all right, little one," he assured her, patting her on the arm. "We all have bad days. You will do much better next time."

Tabitha nodded miserably, her face and neck red with embarrassment. She walked over to look out the tall windows down toward the river. As Sarah swept by her on Señor Alfredo's arm, she saw that her face and neck still were flushed.

When it was Tabitha's turn to play for him to dance with Abigail, though, a pleasure he always saved for last, Sarah was relieved that she played better than she had danced.

Sarah edged over toward the door, then glanced back at Señor Alfredo, swooping around the room with Abigail, oblivious to what anyone else was doing. She went into the hallway, and wandered down the way she had gone last week, stopping in the doorway to Señor Alfredo's quarters. She listened, but there were no ghostly footsteps overhead today.

★ Chapter Eleven ★

Were slaves hidden at Pleasantwood? Uncle Ethan had not answered that question when she had asked it the other day. If they were, how long did they stay before they were shipped home? Where did Uncle Ethan and his men take them to be put on a boat to Africa or the West Indies? And where were the Woodards? The girls had not seen the family once since beginning their lessons. Were they on a boat somewhere helping the slaves return to their homes?

Again using the back stairs, Sarah entered the second floor hallway and wandered along it, glancing into rooms that took her breath away with their rich fabrics and colors.

Then she went on down to the kitchens and asked the same black woman she had met there last week for a drink of water. When she had finished, she went outside and sat down on the back stoop to wait for Sam and the carriage.

Suddenly, Sam came careening up the driveway, so fast that Sarah thought the carriage might turn over. He pulled up before the back of the house and sat pretending he didn't know she was there.

She walked over to the carriage. "Sam, where have you been?" she asked. "I thought you waited down at the stables until time to go home."

"Well, Miss Sarah, I . . . uh . . . had a little errand to do for the governor. I'm sorry if you've been waiting long."

"Oh, no, the others are still dancing. I just got bored and came out here to wait in the sunshine."

"Yes, ma'am," he said politely, but she could tell his interest was somewhere else. Where had he been for the last hour and a half?

Sarah climbed up on the wheel and into the seat beside him. "Are you involved in it, Sam?" she asked softly.

He looked quickly at her, then away across the fields.

"Miss Sarah, I just do what I'm told, by the governor, by Colonel Armstrong, by my pa. I'm not involved in anything, ma'am, except trying to learn a trade and earn a—"

"Sam," she interrupted, "I know all about it. The secrets are safe with me."

"Miss Sarah, I . . ."

"All ready to go?" the militiaman who had ridden over with them today asked from the driveway below.

"Yes, Sergeant," Sam answered, touching his hat brim politely.

Sarah glanced toward the house and saw her cousins coming down the steps. She let the sergeant help her down from her high seat and into the carriage. Abigail and Tabitha followed.

"Sarah, where have you been?" Abigail asked. "Señor Alfredo was asking for you."

"He was? He hardly knows I'm alive when he's dancing with you, Abigail, and so long as the music goes on, I suspect he is hardly aware of Tabitha either. Why would he ask for me?"

"Oh, I suppose he just wondered where you had gone. But it's a big place, Sarah. It would be easy to get lost there and never be seen again!"

"You really should stay close to us, Sarah," Tabitha put in, "for, though I don't think any of the servants are much interested in our whereabouts, I'm sure the Woodards wouldn't want us wandering around their house too freely while they're away."

"Where are they?" Sarah asked.

"Señor Alfredo told us today that they are in Philadelphia visiting Mrs. Woodard's sister, and they won't be back for at least two more weeks, just in time for the Governor's Ball,"

Abigail informed her. She nudged her sister. "Didn't he, Tabitha?"

"Ummmmm," Tabitha commented.

Abigail rolled her eyes in disgust. "If I ever get that stupid expression on my face because of some boy, just shoot me and put me out of my misery!" she said.

"That's the way you look, 'Gail, when Señor Alfredo dances with you," Tabitha retorted.

"I do not!" Abigail said indignantly.

"I think you are in love with Señor Alfredo," Tabitha went on, "and he's at least twice your age! What would Ma and Pa say to that?"

"You'd better not suggest it to them!" Abigail warned.

"If I thought you had mentioned Seth's riding with me to Pa, I would, dear sister!"

Abigail stuck her nose in the air and turned to stare out the window.

How silly her cousins were, Sarah thought. Why, if they only knew the things that were going on around here, they'd—

Suddenly, the carriage stopped with a jolt that threw all three girls off their seats and into a heap on the floor.

Sarah untangled herself quickly, raised up, and looked out the window. "Sam, what? . . ." she began, but she stopped as she saw three men on horseback talking to him.

"Sir, I drove these ladies to their music and dancing lessons at Pleasantwood Plantation," she heard Sam say, "and now I'm driving them home."

The large man with the red face turned to the others. "Was this the carriage you saw at Wickland?"

"It's mighty like it," the tall, skinny one answered.

"Naw, it was this one!" the third man, a short, burly fel-

93

low, insisted, "and he was driving it. The other fellow wasn't with him, though."

"Whose carriage is this?" the first man asked Sam.

"This is the carriage of Colonel Ethan Armstrong, carrying his daughters and his niece," the sergeant said, "and I would suggest that you let it pass!"

"Did you hear that, men?" the red-faced man asked. "He 'suggests' we let this carriage pass. What do you think?"

The other two laughed unpleasantly.

"Oh, we'll let it pass, all right, but if it should end up in a ditch farther along the road, don't blame us!" the tall man said.

"We'll be sorry as the next man to see such a fancy carriage turned over and its elegant passengers rolling in the mud!" the burly fellow sneered.

Fear crawled down Sarah's spine. She had no doubt that the threat was real.

"What are we going to do?" Abigail whispered, crawling back onto the seat.

"We have no money," Tabitha said, as she joined her. "Maybe if we offered them our jewelry. . . ."

"Our jewelry?" Abigail scoffed. "My glass beads and your enameled pin? And Sarah isn't even wearing any!"

"Well, it was the only thing I could think of right now, 'Gail!" Tabitha moaned.

The red-faced man rode back and stuck his head in the window. "Oh, my, my, gentlemen, what have we here?" he said.

A shot rang out, and Sarah heard a bullet whiz behind the man's head. He jerked it out of the window.

"Stand away from that carriage!" the sergeant ordered.

The men looked at the militiaman, then at each other.

94

Finally, the red-faced man motioned for the other two to follow, and they all rode off down the road ahead of the carriage.

Tabitha and Abigail threw their arms around each other and began to cry.

"Hold on, ladies!" Sam called. "I'm going to do my best to get you home before dark!"

The carriage jolted along behind the racing horses, the girls holding onto the seats for dear life. At every bend, Sarah expected to find the three men waiting in ambush, especially as they neared Wickland Plantation with its three crowns carved into the gateposts. But, before long, they were turning down Palace Street and then down Nicholson, and they had seen nothing more of their tormentors.

"Sam, are you going to tell Uncle Ethan about this?" Sarah asked as the sergeant helped them to the street.

"Why, yes, ma'am," Sam answered, surprised she asked.

"Of course, we are," the sergeant agreed. "I'd say, when the colonel is through with those men, they'll think twice before they accost this carriage again on the Jamestown Road!"

"We won't ever be on the Jamestown Road again," Abigail wailed, "when Ma hears what happened out there today!"

"Well, 'Gail, I can't say I ever want to be!" Tabitha said.

"Thank you," Sarah said to Sam and the sergeant. "You needn't wait. We will tell my uncle as soon as he comes home about how bravely you both protected us," she promised, hoping to avoid her aunt's overhearing the men's story. She would be sure to forbid any more trips to Pleasantwood if she did, and Sarah was determined to find out more about what was happening at the big house. "I'm sure my uncle will be very grateful," she added.

She was relieved to see the men touch their hat brims respectfully and drive off toward the stable.

"Ethan, I will never let these girls travel that road again!" Aunt Charity declared at supper that night.

The sergeant had come by to make sure the colonel knew about the disaster they had so narrowly escaped that afternoon and, Sarah thought, his own role in their safe return home. He had made no effort to keep her aunt from hearing all the nasty details.

"All right, Charity," Uncle Ethan agreed. "I understand your concern. In fact, I share it. However, they came to no harm, thank the good Lord, and Sam and Sergeant Nelson performed their duties admirably."

"So our music and dancing lessons are over," Abigail said desolately.

Her mother patted her hand across the table. "We'll find someone here in Williamsburg who can teach you, dear," she assured her.

As she watched tears gather in Abigail's big blue eyes,

Sarah knew her cousin didn't want just music and dancing lessons. She wanted them from Señor Alfredo. "What if Señor Alfredo would come here to instruct us?" she suggested.

"Oh, I'm sure he would!" Tabitha put in excitedly. "He has no carriage, but if you would let Sam pick him up, bring him here, and then take him home, Pa, I'm sure he would come!"

"It's a long drive, Tabitha," her father said. "That would mean a double trip each day—over there and back to pick him up and again to take him home."

"It's no use, girls," Abigail said dejectedly. "We have no ballroom, and our parlor just isn't big enough for such dancing as we do at Pleasantwood."

Sarah recalled the sweeping movements Abigail and Señor Alfredo made around the big dance floor and knew she was right. There certainly was no room in the snug brick house for such dancing! In fact, no matter who taught them, where would they practice? The only place she knew of in Williamsburg with a ballroom was the Governor's Palace itself. Of course, there might be others of which she was unaware.

"I'm sorry, girls, but I cannot justify risking your lives for the sake of a few music and dancing lessons!" Aunt Charity said firmly.

"May I please be excused?" Abigail asked in a small voice that Sarah knew meant she was close to tears. At her mother's nod, Abigail laid her napkin beside her plate and walked quickly into the hallway. Sarah heard her running up the stairs to her room.

"Ma, isn't there anything you can do?" Tabitha begged. "I'm afraid 'Gail's heart is broken, and she was doing so marvelously well with both her dancing and her playing. Even if

★ Chapter Twelve ★

Sarah and I can't have lessons, is there any way you can arrange for 'Gail to continue?"

"I told her we would find someone here in town," Aunt Charity reminded them.

"But, Ma, it's just not the same!" Tabitha protested. "Señor Alfredo is such an excellent teacher, and 'Gail . . . well, you should see them dancing together."

"I will not allow you on that road again, Tabitha," Aunt Charity repeated in a quiet voice that meant the discussion was over.

When they went upstairs to bed, Sarah heard Abigail sobbing in her room. She hesitated, then went on down the hall to the room she shared with Megan. She didn't think Abigail would welcome her intrusion, especially since she had no solution to offer.

She had shared Abigail's room when she had first come to Williamsburg. Abigail had constantly reminded her to use only this little drawer in the dresser and that small space in the closet, to stay out of her chair and her things, to make sure she lay on her edge of the bed. Finally, Sarah had moved down the hall to share Megan's room.

Meggie might be a pest sometimes, she thought, climbing into bed beside her little cousin, but there was no doubt in Sarah's mind that she wanted her with her, sometimes more than Sarah wanted to be there! Sarah smiled fondly at the little girl, already half asleep on her side of the big bed.

Sarah lay down and pulled the thick comforter over her, feeling her bones sinking tiredly into the goose feathers beneath her. It had been a long day, full of terrifying and frustrating events.

Suddenly, she remembered Sam careening recklessly up the driveway when it was time for them to go home. Where had he been? He usually waited for them in the stable area at Pleasantwood. At least, she had thought he did. Where had he been today?

Hadn't the men who stopped them on the road said something about Sam and the carriage being at Wickland that afternoon? And Sam had not denied being at Wickland. He simply had said he had taken the girls to Pleasantwood, and was now taking them home.

Had Sam been at Wickland that day? And if he had, why had he been there? He had told Sarah that he had an errand to do for Governor Henry.

Sarah knew Wickland was the name of the plantation owned by George Burwick, the man who had sold Dulcie and Sam to the slave trader who had then taken them to the Carolina cotton plantation. Sam had pointed it out to her on one of their trips, and he had said the man who had tried to run them down on the Jamestown Road that first time was the owner of Wickland.

George Burwick was a cruel and greedy man who, according to Marcus, would sell his grandmother for a farthing. Was he into something—perhaps the slave smuggling!—that had led the governor to assign Sam some mysterious errand on his property?

Sarah could hear Megan breathing deeply beside her. Outside, the cedar tree sighed in the wind as rain beat against the windowpanes. Sarah sighed with it, knowing she could find answers to none of her questions tonight. She let herself sink farther into the featherbed, and soon fell into a restless sleep, haunted by her memories of the day.

Friday morning, Sarah awoke to the tempting odor of sausage frying and hot bread baking.

★ Chapter Twelve ★

"I hope Hester is fixing fried apples, too," Megan said from over by the dresser, where she was trying to tuck stray curls back into her dark braids from yesterday.

Sarah jumped out of bed and pulled on her brown dress and a clean apron. "Let me rebraid those, Meggie," she offered. "Aunt Charity would have a fit if she saw that mess!"

Quickly, she undid the long braids, combed them, rebraided them neatly, and tied them with pale blue ribbons to match Meggie's dress. "Now, even the queen of England would be pleased with your appearance!" she teased.

"American Patriots don't care what old Queen Charlotte thinks! Or old King George, either!" Megan retorted, running down the hallway ahead of her. "Beat you to the apples!" she challenged, already halfway down the stairs.

When they took their places at the table with Tabitha, Abigail, and Aunt Charity, Sarah noted an empty place.

"Where's Pa?" Megan voiced Sarah's own silent question.

"He had to go out last night," Aunt Charity explained, her eyes on the platter of sausage she was passing. She picked up the bowl of steaming apples. "Now, girls, I will need a lot of help from you today," she said, changing the subject. "Thanksgiving is upon us, and I want to invite Miss Jamison to eat with us, since she has nobody here in Williamsburg."

"How nice, Ma!" Tabitha exclaimed, but Sarah saw Abigail make a face and roll her eyes.

"Some don't keep the Thanksgiving traditions of our ancestors, honoring God for His provision," she continued, "but next to Christmas, Thanksgiving is my favorite holiday. Hester and I will have our hands full with the cooking, though, and I will want you three girls to see to the cleaning and decorating."

"Four," Megan corrected.

"What, dear?" her mother asked absently.

"I said, 'four,'" the little girl repeated. "I am a girl, and I can help! I 'specially like decorating," she added with a grin that Sarah couldn't help returning.

"When will Pa be back?" Abigail asked, and Sarah noticed that she still looked sad this morning, her eyes swollen and puffy from her tears last night.

Tabitha and Megan stopped eating to listen to their mother's answer.

Aunt Charity laid down her fork and leaned toward them. "Your pa had to go on one of his errands last night," she said clearly. "I have no idea where he went or when he will be back. We will just pray for his safety, and welcome him home when he gets here," she instructed.

Thanksgiving came, and Miss Jamison with it. The house smelled of beeswax and spices when the tutor came in, complimenting everything from the gleaming floors and furniture to the centerpiece of leaves and fruit on the table, surrounded by Sarah's mother's flowered china.

When they were seated around the table, Aunt Charity said, "Now, let's all join hands and each one thank God for some special blessing this past year. You begin, Miss Jamison, and I will close the prayer."

As Megan slipped her hand into Sarah's, Sarah wondered what there was to be thankful for that wouldn't be overshadowed by her uncle's uncertain circumstances.

"Thank you, Heavenly Father, for these good friends who have invited me to share their bounty on this

Thanksgiving Day," Miss Jamison said primly.

Abigail expressed appreciation for their music and dancing teacher, and Tabitha thanked God for her family, but Sarah was sure she heard her add the name of Seth Coler under her breath.

"I'm thankful Sarah came back to live with us," Megan said earnestly, and then it was Sarah's turn.

Suddenly, she remembered that evening on the trail in Kentucky a few months ago when she had made friends with God, just like her pa and Marcus said they had done. Since then, all the emptiness that had been inside her had been filled with a peace that not even the war or her uncle's disappearance could disturb.

"I am thankful for Jesus, who died on the cross so that we all might have forgiveness for our sins and be a part of God's family," she said shyly, feeling her face turn red. But when Aunt Charity closed the prayer and Sarah looked up, she found her aunt smiling at her, one of those special smiles that bestowed the rare warmth of her approval.

Sarah's eyes kept straying to Aunt Charity as they passed and savored the baked hen, dressing, and vegetables. She noticed that, though Aunt Charity ate almost nothing herself, she kept piling food on Miss Jamison's plate and insisting that she eat. When the scrawny little woman had finished her third piece of pumpkin pie, and protested that she "couldn't eat another bite," Sarah saw her aunt slip half of a pumpkin pie into a basket of leftovers for Miss Jamison to take home with her.

Sarah smiled, thinking that even though her aunt presented a cold exterior to the world, she had a heart as kind as Ma's when you came right down to it.

The day of thanksgiving to God for their bounty had

come and gone, Sarah thought, and still their prayers for her uncle had not been answered. There had been no word from him since the night he had left. Sarah was convinced that he had met with some terrible fate, either on one of his war errands or as he tried to intercept another boatload of smuggled slaves.

Then she had another thought: What if he had gone to Wickland to investigate the three men who had threatened them on the Jamestown Road, and George Burwick had locked him up in some dungeon or had him killed?

Sarah knew her aunt must be frantic with worry, but she went about running the household as though nothing were wrong.

They all tried to pretend this was so, as they went about their daily chores, picked at the food Hester prepared, and waited.

Nearly a week after Thanksgiving, Sam came to the back door, asking for Aunt Charity. He wouldn't come inside, so Aunt Charity went out to talk with him.

The girls watched from a parlor window, and could see them talking earnestly on the back stoop, but they could not tell what was being said.

Aunt Charity came back inside, her face pale, her blue eyes wild. She wouldn't look at any of them. She went straight into her husband's study and closed the door.

I know Pa's dead!" Abigail wailed, as the minutes went by and her mother did not reappear.

Megan began to cry, and Tabitha put her arms around her. "Hush, Meggie. 'Gail's just upset. Pa's not dead, or Ma would have told us."

Sarah wasn't so sure about that. Her aunt was one of those people who tried to cope with everything herself.

The minutes dragged on as the girls waited in the parlor, only Meggie's sniffling and the ticking of the clock on the mantel breaking the silence.

As the clock began to strike the hour, they heard the door to the study open. Aunt Charity came into the room. She was calm and controlled, though Sarah noticed her slim fingers twisting the handkerchief in her hands.

"Girls, your father has been located," she said. "He is in prison."

"Prison!" Tabitha gasped. Megan began to cry again, and

Abigail stared at her mother in horror.

Sarah saw her aunt swallow hard, then look off into the fire burning in the fireplace. When she turned back to them, her voice was as steady as the flames.

"Yes, prison," she said firmly. "He has been captured by the British. They want to hang him as a spy."

"A spy!" Tabitha and Abigail said together.

"Hang him!" Sarah breathed.

Megan began to sob aloud, and ran to bury her face in her mother's skirt. Sarah saw Aunt Charity put both arms around the little girl.

"I didn't want to tell you," she went on calmly, "but you would hear it, anyway. The trial will be the talk of Williamsburg for weeks to come. Of course, Governor Henry, Thomas Jefferson, and others will do everything they can to secure his release."

Sarah wasn't surprised about the British wanting to hang her uncle. He was a devout and dedicated Patriot, determined to defeat the redcoat army and make the new American states free of British rule. He had been a thorn in the flesh of the British since the war began.

"Where is Uncle Ethan?" she asked.

"They have taken him to Fort Chiswell," Aunt Charity answered. "It is a British post near the Chiswell lead mines over in Wythe County. I hope and pray that Ethan . . ." She stopped, leaving them to imagine what she left unsaid.

"Have they hurt him?" Abigail whispered.

"Is he cold and hungry?" Sarah asked.

Tabitha put both hands over her face and Sarah saw her shudder. Megan's sobs grew louder.

"Hush, Megan," Aunt Charity said firmly. "I don't know, girls, what the conditions are at Chiswell. I've heard some rumors about how prisoners are treated there, but that's all they are, and I won't dignify them by repeating them."

"Can we see him, Ma?" Tabitha asked. "Can we take him things?"

Aunt Charity straightened her shoulders. "I certainly aim to try, girls," she assured them. "Tomorrow, you may help me fix a basket for your father. Sam has promised to be here at sunrise to drive me to Wythe County. I hope to be back before dark, but if I am not, Tabitha, you will take charge of the household until I return."

Early the next morning, when Sarah heard her aunt moving around in her room, she slipped out of bed and dressed quietly, not wanting to awaken Megan. It might be best if the little girl slept through her mother's leaving, she thought as she came into the hallway just as Tabitha and Abigail emerged from their rooms.

Downstairs in the kitchen, Tabitha and Abigail made it clear that they wanted to be the ones helping Hester pack the basket of food, each of them tucking in things they knew their father especially liked. Sarah, not wanting to intrude, stood watching, handing them things when she could.

The sun was just creeping down Nicholson Street when they heard the carriage pull up out front.

Aunt Charity folded a cover from her bed, tucked it into the basket, and bent quickly to kiss each of the girls on the cheek, even Sarah. "Pray for him, girls!" she said. She turned and left the house. She handed Sam the basket, and let him help her into the carriage.

"Wait!" Sarah called. She ran back inside, grabbed the big black Bible from Uncle Ethan's desk, and ran back outside with it. "He will want something to read," she explained, suddenly shy and uncertain about her impulsive act.

Aunt Charity smiled at her. "Thank you, Sarah," she said, taking the Bible from her. "I know he will appreciate your thoughtfulness."

The girls stood watching the carriage pull away from the house, turn the corner, and disappear down Palace Street.

"Well, we might as well go inside and help Hester with breakfast," Tabitha said, taking charge as her mother had told her to do.

"Do you think Ma will be all right?" Abigail asked doubtfully. "You know the dangers on the Jamestown Road, and she has only Sam to protect her. I don't know what we would have done the other day without the sergeant and his gun. Do you suppose Sam has a gun?"

"I think it's against the law for him to carry a gun," Sarah said, "but that doesn't mean he may not have one tucked under the seat or under his shirt."

"I hope he does!" Abigail said vehemently. "I hope he has two guns and a sword and—"

"Girls, do you want bacon and eggs or biscuits and jelly?" Tabitha interrupted briskly. "We aren't going to fix both this morning, and we're going to eat in the kitchen. There's no need to mess up the dining room just for us!"

When they had finished their biscuits and cleaned up the kitchen, Megan wandered downstairs in her long nightgown, rubbing her eyes sleepily. "Where's Ma?" she asked. "I want her to fix . . ." Then Sarah could see memory coming back. "She's gone, isn't she?" Megan wailed.

"Meggie, Ma had to take some food and covers to Pa. You don't want him to be cold and hungry in prison, do you?" Tabitha said.

"I don't want him to be there at all!" Megan cried. "I

want him right here at home, and Ma with him!"

"She'll be back before we know it, Meggie," Sarah put in, offering the little girl some biscuits and grape jelly, hoping to head off the tears she could see threatening. She wished she could make that same promise about Uncle Ethan, but who knew how long he would be in that dreadful place, or what might happen to him when his trial was completed?

"The sun's going to shine, I believe," Hester said from her place behind the ironing board, where she was pressing the last wrinkles from the ruffles and flounces of the finished ball gowns. "Madame Armstrong will have pleasant weather for her journey, at least."

It was the most positive thing Sarah had ever heard the sour old woman say, and she turned to smile at her gratefully. Hester bent over her ironing, her face wearing its usual frozen look. Sarah was relieved, for she often had thought Hester's face might crack, like old china, if she smiled.

"Will you play with me, Sarah?" Megan asked plaintively when she had finished her biscuit and jelly and refused a second one. "Ma made me a new dress for my doll out of a scrap from my ball dress. We could dress Tiger up in it."

Sarah laughed. "The last thing that cat wants is to wear a dress, new or old," she said, knowing her protests—and Tiger's—would be useless. The striped, half-grown cat would be wearing a dress before this day was over!

"First, you may run the dust mop over the floors and the feather duster over the furniture, while I prepare menus for dinner and supper and straighten the parlor," Tabitha said, sounding exactly like her mother.

Abigail rolled her eyes at Sarah as she went past on her way to the closet to get the dust mop. Sarah grinned, reaching for the duster.

"I'll go get my doll dress," Megan said determinedly, sounding every bit as much like Aunt Charity as her sister.

By the time their work was done and the tutor had come and gone, Hester had a light dinner on the table.

After they had finished their meal, Tabitha insisted they all begin the afternoon cross-stitching the samplers they had been assigned by Miss Jamison, and she started Megan to stitching the alphabet. Then Abigail played the harpsichord while Sarah and Tabitha practiced the minuet as best they could in the limited space of the parlor.

Noticing Megan watching forlornly, holding her doll dress, Sarah took the little girl's hands and pulled her up from the sofa and into a wild dance around the room. Then she helped her dress an indignant Tiger in the doll dress. By the time they had relieved the cat of his burden and put him back outside, supper was ready.

Tabitha had them bow their heads and offer thanks before she filled their bowls with stew from the steaming tureen. Then she sliced the crusty bread and passed it around the table. They were just finishing their first helpings when they heard the carriage, and all ran to the front door.

Aunt Charity looked tired, and her blue eyes obviously had shed tears that day.

"Well, girls," she began briskly, "is everything all right here?"

"Of course, Ma," Tabitha answered, "but what about Pa?"

"Did you see him?" Megan cried.

"Did you give him the food and the cover?" Abigail added.

Sarah noticed that Aunt Charity's smile did not reach her

eyes, and she did not look directly at them as she answered. "I didn't actually get to see him, but the guard assured me that he is all right." She busied herself with removing her cloak and hanging it in the hall closet. "And he promised me that he would deliver the basket to your pa himself. I tucked the Bible under the cover, Sarah," she added.

"Come have some supper, Ma," Tabitha suggested, taking her mother's hand and pulling her toward the dining room.

"Later, perhaps," Aunt Charity said. "I'm really not hungry right now, dear. Now, tell me how your day has gone."

As the girls filled their mother in on the uneventful happenings of the day, Sarah sat wondering how her uncle really was being treated in that British prison. Was he warm and fed from the contents of their basket by now, or was the "helpful" guard enjoying their provisions, as Uncle Ethan shivered in the cold, his stomach aching with emptiness? Would he even be given his Bible to read in the long, lonely hours that stretched ahead of him?

Sarah spent a restless night, filled with dreams of her uncle, hurt and dying, in a cold, damp dungeon without food or water.

She awoke the next morning, knowing she had to talk with Marcus. Her uncle was an intelligent man. He had outwitted the British many times, coming and going through their lines almost when and where he wished. What had happened this time that they had caught him? What had he been attempting to do? And was he hurt? Surely Marcus could tell her.

After church services and dinner, she asked permission to visit the gardens at the palace, but halfway there, she realized that Marcus, on Sunday, was likely to be at home with his family. She turned and headed for Raccoons Chase.

Before she reached the little house, she heard Dulcie singing. She stood on the stoop, listening to the trills of some melody Dulcie must have brought with her from the islands years ago. Marcus was right. Surely nobody in the world had a voice like Dulcie! What a treat the governor's guests would enjoy at the ball!

Finally, she knocked on the door. When Marcus answered, Dulcie was seated in the rocking chair before the fireplace. She held up a soft, rose-colored material for Sarah to see. "My new dress for the Governor's Ball," she said. "Can you believe I be going to entertain the guests?"

Sarah smiled at her and nodded. "You sing beautifully, Dulcie."

"Marcus bought me this to make me a new dress," she went on, stroking the material lovingly with one work-worn dark hand. "I'm putting in long sleeves so my mark won't show," she added matter-of-factly.

"What mark, Dulcie?" Sarah asked. She didn't remember seeing any mark on Dulcie, except the mark of hard work on her hands and the mark of trouble in her eyes.

Dulcie held up one arm, and Sarah gasped. Burned into the skin of her lower right arm was a mark that she had seen somewhere before.

"It is the mark of Wickland, of Basil Burwick," Marcus said bitterly. "He has all his slaves branded with it to show they belong to him."

Then Sarah remembered. It was the triple crown that marked the gateposts of Wickland Plantation and the carriage that had tried to run them off the road that day. She shuddered and looked away from the puckered scar. How horrible to brand someone like cattle! The more she learned of slavery, the more she wanted to do something to destroy it, like Uncle Ethan. Which reminded her of why she had come.

"Marcus, I came to ask if you could tell me about Uncle

Ethan," she began. "Was he hurt when the British captured him? And what happened that they were able to take him? He has always outsmarted them before."

Marcus motioned for her to sit in the straight-backed chair. He went over to stir the fire burning cozily in the fireplace. He threw another log onto the fire.

"Miss Sarah, he said finally, "it wasn't the British."

"But they've got him!" she argued. "Aunt Charity said he's in that British prison over at Fort Chiswell. She tried to see him, but they wouldn't let her."

Marcus nodded. "I know, missy. The British have him, but it wasn't the British who captured him."

"Who, then, Marcus? Who was it? And why?"

"It was the slave smugglers. Colonel Armstrong told me you knew about it, Miss Sarah, so I reckon I'm not talking out of turn when I tell you we intercepted them just as they were unloading a new shipment at a landing on the James River. But they were watching for us this time, and they had reinforcements. A band of men came riding out of the woods. There was a terrible fight, and Colonel Armstrong was captured."

"But how did the British get him? Were they helping the smugglers?"

He shook his head. "No, ma'am. The smugglers must have turned him over to the British later, probably for a price."

"Was he hurt, Marcus?" she asked, dreading the answer.

"I don't think so, Miss Sarah," he answered. "Least ways, he wasn't the last I saw of him. He was fighting those rascals like a tiger!" He grinned at her, then sighed. "There were just too many of them, and too few of us."

"Oh, Marcus, what can we do?"

★ Chapter Fourteen ★

"Miss Sarah, we can't do anything. The British keep a lot of important prisoners in that fort. We couldn't even get close to it. And believe me, we have tried!"

"But we can't just let him stay there!" she protested, tears threatening. "Who knows what kind of conditions he's having to endure! They may even be torturing him! You know how involved he is in the Patriot cause. He likely knows things the British want to know."

He patted her hand. "I know, Miss Sarah, I know," he said, and she could see that he was as distressed about it as she was. "Governor Henry has assured me that they are doing everything they can. They're trying to trade one of the British we have taken prisoner for him. We'll just have to wait, Miss Sarah, and pray!"

"I have prayed, Marcus! I have prayed and prayed! Why hasn't God answered?" she blurted. "Isn't He listening? Or does He just not care?"

"Oh, honey, you know God always listens. And He cares. The Good Book says, 'Cast all your cares on Him, for He careth for you,'" he reminded her. "He just works in mysterious ways sometimes."

Sarah remembered the prayers she had said two years ago, asking God not to let her family move from Miller's Forks to Kentucky. She had spent a whole year wallowing in bitterness because she had thought God did not answer those prayers. Then, when Nate finally brought her back to Virginia and she had visited the little brick house in Miller's Forks, she had realized that it was just an empty house without her family. God had answered her prayers. He had not let her leave home, for she had taken it with her.

She sighed. She supposed God had some answer to her prayers about Uncle Ethan, too. She just couldn't see it yet.

Marcus patted her hand. "He will answer, Miss Sarah, in His own time and in His own way. Just be patient."

"I'll try, Marcus," she promised, getting up to leave.

As she reached for the doorknob, Sarah realized that Sam was not there. The little house only had one room. As big as Sam was, it would be impossible to miss him.

"Where is Sam?" she asked.

"Oh, he's off in the woods somewhere," Marcus answered. "That boy! Ever since he lived with those Indians, he's been about half Indian himself! It's all I can do to keep him on the job at the palace. But he's a good worker when he's there," he admitted.

She nodded. "He's a good carriage driver, Marcus," she said, remembering the expert way he had handled the horses as they raced home the day the three men had threatened them on the Jamestown Road. "And he's intelligent. I'd a lot rather talk with Sam than try to carry on a conversation with my empty-headed cousins! All Abigail wants to talk about is fashions and dancing and Señor Alfredo, our instructor. And all Tabitha is interested in is Seth Coler and getting married!'"

"Well, Sam's not interested in any of those things!" Marcus agreed, laughing.

"But nobody will let Sam and me talk," she went on in disgust. "They say it 'isn't proper.' "

Marcus smiled at her. "Honey, most people would say it isn't proper for you and me to be such good friends, either. But that doesn't change things, does it?"

She shook her head, smiling back at him.

"It's no use butting your head against a stone wall, Miss Sarah," he continued. "Sometimes it takes a long time to change how people think."

"But, Marcus, does that mean we should not fight something we know is wrong?"

"No, ma'am," he said. "It just means we need to pick our fights carefully. Now, slave smuggling—that's something we can and should fight, because it makes such misery for folks. But what people think about what's proper and what's not just doesn't amount to much in the long run. Someday, all that will change, anyway, I suspect. Meanwhile, you and I will just keep on being friends!"

"Yes, Marcus, you and I will always be friends," she agreed, sure of it. They had been through too much together to ever return to being just acquaintances. Sarah said good-bye to Dulcie and left the little house.

She knew Marcus was right about Uncle Ethan, too. She ought to just pray and let God take care of him. Her uncle always said she was too quick to try to take matters into her own hands. But she had grown to love Uncle Ethan second only to her own father. Just the thought of him being mistreated by the British made her blood run cold. Surely there was something she could do!

As the gray early December days dragged by, though, nothing came to mind. She prayed for her uncle many times each day, and she knew her aunt and cousins did, too. One day, she kept telling herself, he would walk up that brick walk and through that front door. Until then, she supposed, they would just keep on praying.

Preparations for the Governor's Ball went on. Aunt Charity had decided that she would not deny the girls the privilege of attending, although her heart wasn't in it now, with her husband in prison.

"Are you going to dress in black like a widow, Ma?" the

always fashion conscious Abigail asked.

"No, dear, I will not assume the role of widow while my husband is alive, no matter where he is!" Aunt Charity declared vehemently. "The dark blue I had planned to wear still is appropriate," she said firmly.

Then the night arrived, and the household was a flurry of girls, ruffled petticoats, whispery silk dresses, curls, and ribbons. Even Sarah's poker-straight hair had been coaxed into curls that fell to her shoulders, tied with a ribbon the color of her emerald green dress.

Then there were last minute practices of dance steps and curtsies, and reminders of manners. Finally, they were ready, and Aunt Charity announced that they would take the carriage to the palace, though it was well within walking distance.

"It's cold out, girls, and anyway, I don't want us to soil our dainty slippers," she explained.

The carriage pulled around to the front of the house, and Sarah was surprised to see Sam perched in the driver's seat, dressed in the governor's livery.

"Why, Sam, you look . . . beautiful!" Sarah blurted, unable to think of a better description.

He smiled down at her. " 'Handsome,' Miss Sarah," he corrected. "It's you and your cousins who are beautiful." Then a look of embarrassment came over his face.

"Governor Henry said I could pick you all up before I started helping guests in and out of their carriages," he quickly changed the subject. He got down to help her, then her aunt and cousins, into the carriage.

"Megan, you are rumpling my dress!" Abigail warned. "I don't know why you have to sit over here with Sarah and me. You could squeeze in there between Ma and Tabitha."

Sarah put her arm around the little girl. "I like having you sit here close to me, Meggie," she whispered in her ear. "In your pretty yellow dress, you look just like a ray of sunshine on this dark December night!"

"Here, trade places with me, 'Gail," Tabitha offered, moving over to sit on the other side of Megan, while Abigail took advantage of the larger space to fluff out her skirts and ruffles.

In less than five minutes, they were at the palace, and Sam was helping them to the ground.

Sarah caught her breath at the sight of the palace, with its wreaths and garlands of evergreens on every door and window and candles glowing everywhere. The front door bore a huge wreath of shiny green holly decorated with red berries and real fruit, along with a dusting of frost that already had accumulated in the chilly air.

The big doors opened, and a servant in livery exactly matching Sam's ushered them into a magnificent entry.

★ Whispers in Williamsburg ★

Sarah surrendered her cloak to a waiting servant, then, taking a deep breath, she followed her cousins into a room thronged with men in powdered wigs and satin coats and women in dresses of every color imaginable.

Sarah made her way through the dancers to the long tables that held every kind of food she had ever heard of—except maybe those flat little cornbread cakes her ma had baked beside the campfire on their journey to Kentucky. Pa and other settlers called them "johnnycakes," but she thought they were really "journey cakes." Anyway, they were about the only food the governor hadn't served tonight!

She took a cup of fruit punch and drank it quickly. Playing games with Megan and her little friends in the children's room was thirsty work, but she preferred it to the silly simpering and posturing of Abigail and some of the other girls.

As Sarah turned to look over the dancers, Abigail swept by on the arm of a handsome militiaman. Then Sarah spotted Tabitha over in the corner, dancing dreamily with her Seth. She looked quickly for Aunt Charity, and found her sitting across the room, talking with two women. She didn't seem concerned about her daughters or her niece at the moment.

Sarah hoped no one would ask her to dance. She didn't care much for it, and her skills were only mediocre. She liked listening to the music, though, and she took a gold-rimmed plate and began to fill it with baked chicken, casseroles, relishes, fancy vegetables and fruits.

There was a fanfare of music from the musicians seated on a raised platform at the far end of the room, and Sarah turned to see the governor standing at the front of the platform.

"Ladies and gentlemen!" Governor Henry said, when the crowd had quieted. "I hope you are enjoying the evening, and now we have a real treat for you. May I please present to you the most beautiful voice I have ever heard!"

He stepped aside, there was another fanfare from the musicians, and a violin and flute began to play softly. Then, from behind an embroidered screen at one side of the platform, Dulcie's extraordinary voice began to weave its way in and out of the melody.

From across the table, Sarah heard a muttered curse. She turned to look straight at a red-faced man with cold, mean eyes. Basil Burwick! The man who had stopped them on the Jamestown Road, the man who had once owned Dulcie and Sam!

She followed his gaze and saw that it was fixed on the screen that hid Dulcie. He swore again. "It's her!" he muttered. "Nobody else can sing like that!"

"Shhhh!" someone ordered.

The man mumbled something under his breath, but he stood silently until the singing was over. Then as the crowd applauded, he strode purposefully to the platform, pushed aside the screen, and dragged Dulcie out before them. "Woman, you will come with me!" he declared.

Two men in uniform came forward. "What are you doing?" one of them asked Burwick roughly.

"I'm claiming my property," the man snarled. "See?" He ripped the sleeve of Dulcie's new rose-colored dress up to the elbow, exposing her arm. "There's my mark!" he announced, holding her arm up for all to see the three-crown mark on its underside. "This woman belongs to me!"

"Now hold on there, Burwick!" the governor said. "This woman is the wife of my gardener. I believe you sold her years ago to a slave trader who, in turn, sold her to a Carolina cotton plantation. I have helped her husband search for her and their son for years. I have found that, in the process of relocating to Kentucky, her owners were killed by Indians. In my opinion, that makes her a free woman."

The man swore again. "That trader never paid me more than a pittance of a down payment on her and her brat! In my opinion," he said sarcastically, "that makes them revert to me! Come on, woman," he snarled, pulling Dulcie across the platform by the arm.

"You will have to prove this in a court of law, Burwick!" Sarah recognized the voice, then saw Thomas Jefferson stride to the platform to stand beside Governor Henry.

"Then sue me!" Burwick snarled, dragging Dulcie onto the dance floor.

Sarah saw the look of utter terror in Dulcie's eyes as he dragged her past, then out the door. Her mind went back to that night at Fort Harrod when the men had captured the frightened woman in the graveyard outside the fort, playing her drum. Would Dulcie go back to the nearly mindless creature she had been then, before the slave Malinda, and then

123

Marcus, had nursed her back to health and sanity?

What would Marcus do? Sarah wondered, looking around for him. Would he risk his life by attacking Burwick to rescue his wife? She knew he would!

She found him in the back garden, catching a breath of air. He smiled when he saw her, then a look of alarm replaced the smile. "What is it, Miss Sarah? You look like you've seen a ghost!"

"Marcus, Burwick's taking Dulcie!" she blurted. "He recognized her singing and dragged her from the platform. He says she still belongs to him."

Marcus's eyes were wild and angry looking. He wheeled around and headed back inside. Sarah ran after him, but he had disappeared by the time she reached the kitchens. She hurried into the room where she had last seen Dulcie.

"We will get her back, Marcus!" she heard the governor promise. "But think, man! What good will you do Dulcie if you are dead or in prison? We will disprove Burwick's claim by law. Tom here will file suit immediately!"

Sarah thought Marcus might hit the governor, he was so distraught. Then she saw him sag, as though all the will had gone out of him.

"I promise you, Marcus," Governor Henry repeated, "we will get her back!"

"Whatever's left of her!" Marcus muttered. "Where's Sam?"

"He was helping people in and out of their carriages," Governor Henry said uncertainly. He turned to one of the soldiers. "Go see if you can find Sam, the big black boy who helps with the carriages. Get him in here before he does something foolish," he ordered. Then he turned to the musicians. "Play!" he commanded.

★ Chapter Fifteen ★

As the music filled the room, the crowd began to talk and mill around, soon filling the hole Dulcie's departure had left. *She is just a slave. Nobody really cares about her,* Sarah thought, *except Marcus and me!* And maybe the governor.

What would Burwick do with Dulcie? Sarah supposed he intended to put her back to work on his plantation. But Burwick was a cruel man. Marcus had said he would sell his own grandmother for a profit, Sam had said he was "mean," and she knew that her uncle agreed with their assessment.

Suddenly she wondered what Burwick would do if Dulcie reverted to the almost mindless creature she had been at the fort. He wouldn't be able to sell her. She would be useless, even a burden to him then. Would he punish her? Would he lock her away in some dungeon at Wickland?

The soldier Governor Henry had sent after Sam came back alone. "He's not out there, Governor," he reported.

"Well, find him!" the Governor ordered.

"It's no use, sir," Marcus put in wearily. "He's run to the woods to hide. We likely won't see him again."

"But, Marcus, can he survive out there?" the Governor questioned. "It's cold now, and food will be scarce. . . ."

"Leave him be," Marcus said. "He's become half Indian. He knows how to survive in the wilderness. Besides, he'd rather starve to death or freeze out there than to go back to Wickland."

The Governor nodded sadly, patted Marcus on the shoulder, and turned away.

Sarah ran to Marcus and threw both arms around his waist. "Oh, Marcus," she said, "I am so sorry!"

He gently untangled her arms. "I know you are, Miss Sarah," he said, his voice so filled with pain that Sarah wanted to weep, right there in front of everybody. She wished there were some way she could make things better, but what could she do?

"Oh, Marcus!" she repeated, tears spilling over and running down her cheeks. She groped for the handkerchief Aunt Charity had insisted she tuck into her left sleeve and wiped her eyes. Then she turned quickly back to Marcus, but he was gone!

She made her way back to the kitchens, where he had been helping with the serving, but there was no sign of him there, either. Where had he gone so quickly? She had only looked away for a moment! Though she searched all the logical places, he had disappeared.

Sarah ran out into the gardens. Perhaps he had gone there, to one of his favorite places, to think, or to pray. Marcus was a praying man, she thought.

"Dear God, please comfort him," she whispered. "And please, please take care of Dulcie! And Sam!"

Marcus was not in the gardens, though, and she returned to the palace, shivering from the cold and from fear for these people she had grown to love. What would become of them now?

If only Uncle Ethan were here! she thought. But he was shut up in that hateful British prison, wasting away, possibly being tortured himself. What on earth was she going to do?

She could almost hear her uncle telling her to wait, to trust in God and in the help of the governor and Mr. Jefferson. "You are the most persistent young lady I have ever known," he had told her on more than one occasion.

But Marcus was her special friend! He had been ever since she had discovered him that day in the stocks on Duke of Gloucester Street. He had comforted her countless times that first year when she was a stranger in Williamsburg. He had helped her find Gabrielle when she needed to say good-bye.

She would do *anything* for Marcus! What could she do against someone like Burwick, though? He was a strong man, a cruel man, and, she supposed as Governor Henry had said, the law was on his side until they proved otherwise. But how long would that take? She had heard of trials that lasted for months or even years! Would Dulcie's mind be completely gone by the time Thomas Jefferson could successfully defend her freedom in a court of law?

What would it take to prove Dulcie no longer belonged to Burwick, to anyone? Her uncle and the other men at Harrodstown had believed that circumstances had made Sam and Dulcie free. If only they had free papers, like Marcus! If only there were some way to prove that the slave trader had paid Burwick! But, so far as Sarah knew, there were no legal papers to support their claims. Burwick wouldn't give Dulcie up easily, now that slaves were bringing nearly 1,000 pounds apiece. And he would do anything he could to get Sam back, too.

Sarah stared unseeingly at the dancers, trying to think of a way to help Marcus get his family back, trying to think of some excuse she could present to Aunt Charity so she could just go home.

"May I have this dance?"

Sarah didn't even look up. "Just leave me alone!" she cried rudely.

"I beg your pardon?" the man said, and Sarah looked up into the blue eyes of a young militiaman who had once been a clerk at Greenhow's Store. She had wondered what had become of him. Once, she would have been happy to see him again.

"I . . . I don't feel like dancing," she stammered. Then she turned and fled back into the children's room.

When she remembered the events of the evening of the Governor's Ball, Sarah couldn't believe how rude she had been to the nice young militiaman she had first met when he was a clerk in Greenhow's Store. All he had done was ask her to dance, she thought, as she draped a spray of cedar over the parlor mantel, and she had fairly bitten off his head!

Just thinking about it sent a warm flush over her face. But she had been so distraught over Marcus, she excused herself. She had been so wrapped up in his pain at losing Dulcie again that she just hadn't been herself. She knew, though, that the excuse would never make it past Aunt Charity's sense of propriety. She was glad her aunt didn't know about it!

Oh, well, she told herself, she probably never would see him again. She didn't even know his name! What did it matter compared to finding some way to help Marcus get his Dulcie back, and some way to bring Sam safely out of hid-

ing, not to mention some way to rescue her uncle from prison?

Sarah sighed. That was a tall order! She hadn't the faintest idea of how she could fill it. She supposed she couldn't. This was one time she would have to do as her uncle and Marcus always advised, and simply trust in the Lord.

She looked around the room with satisfaction. The cedar and candles in the wide windowsills and the nativity set on the mantel gave the room a festive air. And, since the other girls were doing similar things in other rooms, she assumed the whole house soon would have that delightful Christmasy smell and feeling.

Sarah wished she could feel Christmasy, but she just couldn't. Uncle Ethan was away from his family and undergoing who knew what. And Marcus was alone again when he should have had such a happy Christmas with his family together after so many years of separation.

Should she try to visit Dulcie, try to help her understand that Governor Henry and his friends were doing all they could to get her declared legally free so she never could be forced into slavery again?

Maybe Marcus could drive her over there. If they found her in better circumstances than he was imagining, it would make Marcus feel better. And surely seeing her husband would comfort Dulcie.

Oh, dear! Sarah thought. Aunt Charity would never let her go! Hadn't she already forbidden them to travel the Jamestown Road to their music and dancing lessons? She would never give Sarah permission to travel that same road to Wickland, the plantation of the very man who had threatened them the other day!

Maybe Seth or Sergeant Nelson would go with them, she planned desperately, convinced now that she had to go.

"Sarah, have you lost your mind?" her aunt gasped when she made her request, as they settled in the parlor after a satisfying meal of Hester's lamb stew and Sally Lund bread.

"Well, no, ma'am. I hope not, ma'am!" Sarah stammered. From over by the fireplace, she heard Megan giggle, and she glanced over to where the little girl perched on a low stool, stitching doggedly on the squiggly letters of her alphabet sampler.

"Of course, I'll not give you permission to go gallivanting around on the Jamestown Road!" her aunt continued. "After what happened the other day? The very idea, Sarah!"

Abigail looked up from finding her place in the reading the tutor had assigned that morning. "She's just an old slave, Sarah," she said. "Why would you want to visit her?"

"Oh, Abigail!" Tabitha scolded from her place behind her sister, where she was reading over her shoulder. "The rector said just last Sunday that it is the duty of every Christian to have compassion for the less fortunate. And here it is only two days before Christmas! Shame on you, 'Gail!"

Abigail turned to glare at Tabitha, then returned to her book. Sarah knew her cousin's bad mood was partly because Abigail didn't like to read anything unless it had to do with fashions or entertainment. The book of household hints held little interest for Abigail and, for once, Sarah shared her opinion, though Tabitha was so excited about it she couldn't wait for Abigail to finish reading the assigned chapter so she could start.

"I understand your concerns for Marcus and his family, Sarah," Aunt Charity went on, "but I simply cannot let you endanger yourself. It isn't likely that you'd be allowed to see her, anyway, and if you were, what could you do to make things better for her and Marcus?"

"She was so scared, Aunt Charity," Sarah explained. "I thought I might be able to comfort her some way."

Her aunt smiled at her. "You are a kind child, Sarah, even if you are a bit headstrong."

She got up and walked over to stand in front of the fireplace. "I wish I could accommodate your desire to help, Sarah," she said, "but my sister has entrusted you to my care, and I cannot risk your safety, no matter how worthy the cause."

Sarah sighed. It was obvious that her aunt was not going to be persuaded. She would have to find some other way to help Marcus and Dulcie. But how?

"Well, then, may I go visit with Marcus for a few minutes, Aunt Charity?" she asked. "I won't stay long."

Her aunt studied her seriously. "I suppose so," she said finally, "but promise me, Sarah, that you will go straight there and come straight back here before dark."

"Yes, ma'am, I will," Sarah agreed quickly, already on her way to the hall closet to get her cloak.

"May I go with her, Ma?" Sarah heard Megan ask.

She was relieved to hear her aunt reply firmly, "No, dear, you may not." She wanted to talk with Marcus alone.

She found him cutting holly branches in the palace gardens. He looked up when he heard her step beside him, and her heart twisted at the pain she saw in his dark eyes.

"Are you pruning the hollies?" she asked, trying to find a topic of conversation that would not add to his pain. "I thought you did that earlier."

He shook his head. "I'm cutting these branches to make fresh wreaths for the palace. Governor Henry won't tolerate wilting greenery in his house." He stopped with a branch in one hand and the pruners in the other. "What can I do for you?"

Sarah's heart ached. His eyes were so full of hurt! If only she could do or say something to make him feel better! But what could ease the pain of losing his wife again, and so soon after she had been restored to him?

Suddenly, she ran to him and threw both arms around his waist, as she had done at the Governor's Ball. "Oh, Marcus!" she cried. "I just want to do something to help you and Dulcie! But I don't know what to do!"

"There, now, child," he said, returning her hug before he gently untangled her arms. "The governor and Mr. Jefferson are doing everything that can be done, I reckon."

"Don't you just want to go over there and beat up that Burwick?" she asked. "Don't you just want to go get Dulcie and bring her home, no matter what he says?"

"Of course I do, missy! But if I went storming over to

Wickland and brought Dulcie home, I would just make grief for her. Burwick would likely kill me, and take her back. And then she would have nobody."

He went back to cutting branches, stacking them neatly beside the gravel path.

"Marcus," she asked reluctantly, again not wanting to add to his pain, "do you think Burwick will try to sell Dulcie again?"

His mouth twisted. "He would sell her to the first person who comes along with enough money in his pocket. You know, slaves are worth a lot of money these days," he said bitterly.

Sarah had no answer for that. "I asked Aunt Charity to let me go visit Dulcie," she said instead, "but she is afraid for me to travel the Jamestown Road. She says they probably wouldn't let me see her, anyway. Do you think they would?"

"I don't know, Miss Sarah," he answered. "Just leave it be. There's really nothing we can do until Mr. Jefferson gets her some legal document stating that she is free. Just pray Burwick doesn't sell her or that she doesn't completely lose her mind before then."

Sarah didn't know what to say. The misery she saw in the old man's face was more than she could bear. She stood looking over toward the canal, willing her tears not to fall.

"Marcus," she said, still not looking at him, "why does God allow such people to live? Slave owners are wicked, selfish people. Why doesn't God just strike them all dead?"

"Well, honey, some slave owners are wicked, like Burwick, but some of them are simply continuing a way of life created by their fathers and their grandfathers, without ever thinking much about it, I reckon. Governor Henry and Mr. Jefferson own slaves. They don't mistreat them, but they do own them, though I've heard both of them say they believe slavery is wrong."

She nodded. She had heard them say that, too, right here in these gardens.

"I believe, someday, men like Colonel Armstrong and the governor and Mr. Jefferson will cause slavery to be outlawed in America," Marcus went on, staring wistfully off over the gardens. "Then even black men will be able to have their families with them, and when they work for someone else, they will receive just wages for their labors, as I do here from Governor Henry."

He turned back to his work. "Meanwhile, we just have to live as the Good Book says, Miss Sarah, doing good and forgiving those who don't."

She knew all about forgiveness. It was Marcus who had made her aware that to be forgiven, she must forgive, even people who betrayed and hurt her as Gabrielle had done.

"Sometimes God punishes the wicked here on this earth, and sometimes we just have to accept on faith that He will keep His word about that." Marcus continued, "It's like accepting His word in John 3:16 that tells us God loved His rebellious creation so much that He gave His only Son, Jesus, to die for them on that splintery old cross in Jerusalem nearly eighteen hundred years ago."

He laid down the pruners and began to pile the stacks of holly on top of each other. "Since then," he went on, "us old sinners don't have to perish like the truly wicked. We can accept the forgiveness purchased for us by His blood and have everlasting life with Him."

Sarah nodded. "Marcus, when I was back in Kentucky, I talked to God, just as you told me I should. I asked Him to forgive me of my sins. I told Him I believe Jesus died in my place, that I want to be friends with Him like you and Pa. I said I want to trust Him with all my heart, and to acknowledge Him in all my ways, just like it says in those verses you love so much in Proverbs."

"Miss Sarah," he said, straightening his back and looking her directly in the eye, "no matter what happens to you the rest of your life, that is the most important decision you will ever make. You have begun a conscious relationship with your Creator, and nothing can ever separate you from His love. So long as you follow those verses from the third chapter of Proverbs, God will honor His promise to make all your paths straight."

He sighed. "That's what I've tried to tell Sam lately, but he's got some hot blood in him from somewhere. Maybe it's my own youthful folly coming out, or maybe it comes from those steamy islands where his ma was born. But he's full of anger and he wants to take matters into his own hands. Pray for him, Miss Sarah."

"Have you heard from him?" she asked.

He shook his head. "Not a word, but I figure he knows how to survive in the woods after all those months with the Indians. I'm just sorry that it's wintertime. I often wonder if he is cold or hungry. And he was doing so well with the carriages and horses."

"He told me once that he preferred the Indian life to the life he had lived on the cotton plantation," Sarah said. "Maybe he's gone back to the Indians he lived with in Kentucky."

"Well, Sam liked the Indian lifestyle well enough," he agreed, "but he didn't like being anybody's slave. I think he's probably around here somewhere. I reckon he'll turn up one of these days, when he thinks he's safe from Burwick.

136

That man would love to get his greedy hands on such a strong young man! He would bring a pretty price on the slave market."

He picked up his pile of branches and headed toward the palace.

"I'd better be going," Sarah said. "I promised Aunt Charity I'd be home before dark." She started toward the gates, then turned back. "Marcus, if there's anything that I can . . ."

"Just keep praying for my Dulcie," he urged, "and for Sam."

"I will," she promised fervently. "I pray for them all the time, and for you."

He smiled at her, a sad little smile. "Don't worry about ole Marcus, honey. He'll be all right. The good Lord has helped him through many a bad time. You just run along home now."

She stood watching him trudge wearily toward the palace. When he disappeared inside the back door, she turned and hurried from the gardens and into the street by the Palace Green.

Sarah wished she had as much faith as Marcus had. She knew he was right to trust in the Lord the way he did. It was just that she felt there was something she ought to be doing to help. Aunt Charity often said that God used the hands of His people to do His work. But what could she do? "Please show me, Lord!" she whispered.

She was halfway to Nicholson Street when she realized she had to go back. She had to talk to Governor Henry.

Sarah shivered and pulled her cloak more closely about her as she stood before the big front doors of the palace, waiting for someone to answer her knock. The December wind was chill, and the sky was overcast as if it was going to rain—again—but perhaps her shivering was from her dread of facing the governor and asking him to help her.

When the black butler answered the door, dressed in livery like Sam and Marcus had worn the night of the ball, she swallowed hard, told him she was Ethan Armstrong's niece, and asked to see Governor Henry. He bowed slightly and made a gesture that indicated she should come inside.

"Wait here," he said, and he disappeared up the massive staircase.

Sarah's gaze traced the walls of the entry to where they ended far above her head. The stairway and doors were draped with garlands and wreaths of greenery, as they had been for the ball, and she breathed in the spicy scent of evergreens. They really didn't look so wilted to her, but she assumed Marcus was busy somewhere back in the palace making new ones.

Soon, the butler was back, motioning for her to follow him up the stairs. He ushered her into a large room, where Governor Henry sat behind a desk, writing with a quill pen on a sheet of paper. He was not wearing the white powdered wig he had worn at the ball, but wore his brown hair pulled back and tied with a black ribbon.

The butler took her cloak and seated her in a chair in front of the desk.

The governor looked up and smiled at her, his bright eyes kind. "Well, if it isn't Miss Sarah Moore, the niece of my good friend Colonel Armstrong!" he exclaimed. "I was just writing a note to your aunt. My dear, it seems that your uncle has escaped from prison!"

Sarah gasped. "Uncle Ethan has escaped?" she repeated.

He nodded. "We are told that he was on his way to yet another questioning by the British when he managed to overpower his guards and take their keys."

"Praise the Lord!" Sarah breathed. "Is my uncle on his way home? Or will he have to hide out somewhere until . . ." Until when? Would he be a fugitive like Sam, hiding in the woods or some other cold, damp place, without food or shelter, until this war was over?

"We don't know where he is," the governor said. "We assume he has taken refuge with some Patriot family until he can make his way back to Williamsburg."

She nodded. Then a new worry came to her. "If he comes home, will the British come after him?" she asked.

"Oh, they will try to recapture him, Sarah. There's no doubt about that! There are many military secrets the British hoped to torture out of Colonel Ethan Armstrong. But they won't dare come to Williamsburg after him, not with so many Patriot soldiers here."

He reached for the bell pull dangling down the wall behind him. "May I offer you a cup of tea or some hot chocolate? You must be chilled from your walk over here." He smiled at her, and the warmth in his eyes reminded her of Uncle Ethan.

"No, thank you, sir," she answered. She really would have liked a cup of chocolate, but she didn't want to drink it in front of the governor, and she didn't want to put him to any trouble, since she was here to ask a favor.

"Then tell me what has brought you here," he urged. "Were you going to ask my help in freeing your uncle from prison? It seems that won't be necessary now," he said with a pleased smile.

"No, sir, but I do need your help, sir, if I may be so bold as to ask."

"Of course, you may! And I'll do my best to accommodate you," he promised. "What is it you want?"

"I want to go to Wickland Plantation to visit Dulcie, Governor Henry," she blurted. "I think I could bring her some comfort, and reassure her that you and Mr. Jefferson are doing everything you can to get her and Sam declared legally free."

"I will have Marcus take you there tomorrow in my carriage," he assured her.

"But, sir, my aunt won't let me go! She won't even let us continue our music and dancing lessons at Pleasantwood Plantation since we were threatened by Basil Burwick on the Jamestown Road."

The Governor suddenly found something very interesting in the papers on his desk. "Sam told me about that," he mumbled. "I'm so sorry!"

Sarah remembered that, when Sam had come racing up the driveway at the last minute to take them home, he had said he had been running an errand for the governor. She wanted to ask Governor Henry what he had asked Sam to do and if it had involved Wickland Plantation, as Burwick had accused.

"Anyway," she said, "Aunt Charity won't let me go, and . . ."

The governor looked into her eyes with a grin. "And you thought I might persuade her?"

He stood up, and not knowing what else to do, Sarah stood with him. "I will send a note to your aunt, telling her that you will be accompanying my messenger on an errand to Wickland Plantation tomorrow," he promised. "There are some papers to be served on Burwick, and I don't see why Lieutenant Parke can't take them tomorrow. Marcus can drive you, and I will send Sergeant Nelson to guard you. I believe I can assure your aunt that you will be perfectly safe. And I do believe you might do Dulcie some good."

"Oh, thank you, sir!" Sarah said, with a curtsy. "I didn't expect! . . . Thank you!" she babbled.

"You are welcome, Sarah. Marcus has told me of the things you have done for him, and I know how much he and his family mean to you. He is a good man. I, too, am very fond of him."

He came around the desk, took her by the elbow, and ushered her out of the room. "Run along, now. I will send someone around with a note to your aunt this evening, and my carriage will pick you up in front of the Armstrong house at sunup."

"Yes, sir. Thank you, sir," she stammered again. She turned and fled down the stairs, then turned to call, "Good-bye!"

She caught a slight smile on the butler's face as he placed her cloak on her shoulders and opened the door for her.

It was nearly dark when she went through the gate and up the brick sidewalk to the Armstrong's front door. She hoped Aunt Charity would not be displeased.

Sarah hung her cloak in the hall closet and followed the sound of voices to the kitchen.

"We are fending for ourselves this evening, Sarah," her aunt said pleasantly. "Hester isn't feeling well, and I have sent her to bed."

"We're making meat pies!" Megan announced. "I'm rolling out the crust."

"I see you are, Meggie," Sarah answered, noting that Tabitha was mixing dough and Abigail was cutting Megan's crust and placing it in the pans.

"Ma's making potato cakes!" Megan added. "I love potato cakes!"

Sarah reached over and tugged on one of the little girl's braids. "You just like food of almost any kind, Meggie!"

"Just about," Megan agreed cheerfully.

"Aunt Charity," Sarah said then, "I have wonderful news! Uncle Ethan has escaped from prison! Governor Henry says he has likely taken refuge with some Patriot family until he can make his way home."

Aunt Charity's face turned pale and her hands flew to her chest. "Ethan has escaped?" she whispered.

"Yes, ma'am. Governor Henry was going to send you a note, but he gave me the message instead."

"Praise God!" Aunt Charity said, and then she did something Sarah would never have believed. She covered her face with both hands and began to cry, the tears spilling through her fingers.

The three girls began to cry, too, Megan sobbing out loud, and soon Sarah found tears running down her own face.

"Praise the Lord!" her aunt said again, fervently. Then she dried her eyes with her apron, smoothed her hair, and, completely in control again, asked calmly, "How on earth did he manage to escape, Sarah? I was there. That prison was like a fortress!"

"The governor said he overpowered his guards and took their keys. He said the British will try to recapture him, but they will not dare come to Williamsburg after him, once he gets home."

A burnt smell filled the air, and Aunt Charity grabbed for her spatula to pry the stuck potato cakes from the iron skillet. She filled the skillet with water to soak. Megan moaned softly.

"Do you think Pa got the food we packed for him, Ma?" Tabitha asked suddenly. "I've been so afraid that he was cold and hungry."

"Me, too," Sarah said, and Abigail nodded, dashing the last of her tears from her wide blue eyes.

"No, I really don't think he did," Aunt Charity answered. "I didn't want to admit it, but I'm afraid that guard enjoyed the goodies we packed for your father, and I doubt that he even gave him the cover. That's why I didn't try to take him anything else. The British have no love for Ethan Armstrong!"

"Do you think he gave him the Bible, Aunt Charity?" Sarah asked.

"I don't know, dear." Then she brightened. "But he is

out of the hands of the British now, and, if I know Ethan, they will not capture him again. He has been very clever at eluding them in the past. And he is loved by Patriots all over Virginia. I'm sure any of them would take good care of him until he can safely make his way back to us."

Aunt Charity turned to Sarah. "Since everyone else already has a job to do," she said, handing her some money, "I want you to run down to Greenhow's Store and get me some black pepper for the pies and some coffee. I'm completely out of both, and the store will be closing soon."

"Yes, ma'am," Sarah said, heading for her cloak.

"Hurry back!" Aunt Charity called after her. "The streetlights are on, but I don't like your being out after dark!"

Sarah quickly made her way along the darkened streets. Waiting at the foot of the steps to Greenhow's Store to let an elderly lady pass her, she heard a whisper, "John 3:19. Tomorrow night!"

Sarah whirled around. In the glow of the streetlights, she saw a young couple walking hand in hand toward Chowning's Tavern, two men in black suits with white knee stockings approaching from the Palace Green, three women sharing an animated conversation just beyond the steps, and two black men with bundles under their arms, waiting to cross Duke of Gloucester Street. Had one of them whispered the code of the men who fought the slave smugglers? She was sure she had heard it. If none of these had said it, who had?

Was a raid planned for tomorrow night? If so, with her uncle in hiding somewhere between Williamsburg and Fort Chiswell, who would lead it? she wondered.

Who else was involved, besides Marcus and the men she had seen at the little church in Raccoons Chase that night?

Was Lieutenant Parke or Sergeant Nelson one of them? She was pretty sure Governor Henry was, but would he actually lead a raid? She doubted it. He was certainly no coward, but he was needed here to run the government. What if he got killed or captured?

Sarah made her way into the store and purchased the pepper and coffee her aunt wanted. She hurried home, still pondering who had been the whisperer on Duke of Gloucester Street, and who had listened for that cryptic code.

When she had hung her cloak in the closet and carried her purchases back to the kitchen, she found Aunt Charity with an envelope in her hand. Sarah glimpsed the broken seal of red wax. It had to be Governor Henry's note saying he would be sending her to Wickland tomorrow. What would her aunt do? Would she refuse to let her go, even with the governor's soldiers?

"Did you ask him to do this, Sarah?" she asked sternly.

"No, ma'am!" Sarah answered. "Well, I asked him for help, and he offered to send me to Wickland. He said his lieutenant had business there, anyway. And he thinks we will be perfectly safe, with the soldiers and all." She was babbling again, but she couldn't seem to stop.

"I see," her aunt said. She stood there studying the note. Finally, she said, "All right, Sarah, I am going to let you go, since the governor has made all these arrangements. But I will expect you back before dark, and I will tell the lieutenant so!"

Sarah didn't doubt it. "Yes, ma'am," she said meekly, not wanting to say anything that might change her aunt's mind.

As Sarah went to bed that night, she heard the wind moaning through the cedar out back. She shivered, praying that her uncle and Sam were safe and warm, with their stomachs full of a good supper. She fell into a troubled sleep, filled with the cedar's restless whispering that, in her dreams, became the whispered words, "John 3:19. Tomorrow night!"

Christmas Eve dawned cold, under a threatening gray sky, and by the time they were on the Jamestown Road, snowflakes had begun to fall.

Sarah tucked the lap robe under her knees, pulled her cloak around her, and slipped her hands inside it. The hot bricks the governor's servants had provided to warm their feet already were beginning to cool.

"Not a pleasant day for a journey," Lieutenant Parke commented, removing his hat, exposing a nearly bald head, then smoothing his neat gray mustache.

Sergeant Nelson, riding backward beside him on the seat facing Sarah, said, "Oh, I don't know, Lieutenant. I like a little snow, especially at Christmastime."

"I don't mind the snow, if I'm in front of the fireplace with a hot drink in my hands!" The lieutenant's blue eyes twinkled.

Sarah lifted the window shade and looked out. The

James River had taken on the gray color of the sky, with the ground between it and the road already dusted with white. The road ahead of them looked as smooth as the streets of Williamsburg. Then one wheel dropped into a rut, jolting her back to the realization that it was not so smooth as the snow made it appear.

Would this journey to Wickland be as smooth as the governor had assured Aunt Charity it would? Would Burwick let them see Dulcie? Or would he be as stubborn about that as he had proved to be about reclaiming her? Sarah remembered the meanness in the man's cold, narrow eyes, and shivered.

"Are you cold, miss?" the Lieutenant asked. "These carriages are certainly warmer than riding horseback, but they lack the comforts of home. Here, take my robe, too."

She shook her head. "No, sir. I'm all right," she said quickly. Then she added, "Thank you." It was Marcus who must be uncomfortable, out there in the driver's high seat, exposed to the wind and the cold, she thought. How much longer would it be before they reached Wickland?

Suddenly the carriage turned sharply right, and they were traveling down the driveway to Burwick's house. Sarah couldn't resist raising the window shade again to catch a glimpse of the house as they drove up.

Wickland wasn't quite as impressive as the mansion at Pleasantwood. Its grimy red brick rose only two stories high, and there were no wings stretching from side to side, no shrubbery or flower beds to soften its entrance. Behind the house, she could see scattered outbuildings.

Marcus stopped the carriage before a mounting block, and climbed down to open the door for them. His eyebrows, under his hat brim, were powdered with snow, and his face

looked stiff with cold. His dark eyes, though, held a banked light that told Sarah he was eager to find what the day might bring.

"Watch your step, Miss Sarah," he cautioned. "That iron step is wet and slick."

Carefully, holding his hand, she stepped to the ground, her eyes on the thick wooden door of the house. If Burwick chose not to welcome them, they would have no chance of getting inside that door!

Where would Dulcie be? Was she able to perform the duties of a slave—in the kitchen or laundry room, in sewing or weaving for the household? Or had she gone back to the near mindless creature they had discovered a few months ago at Harrodstown? Had they shut her up in some dungeon or attic room until she could be sold to an unsuspecting buyer?

The lieutenant strode ahead and knocked loudly on the door. Before it opened, Sarah and Marcus had joined him on the stoop. She glanced behind her and saw that the sergeant had climbed to the driver's seat of the carriage.

The door opened a crack, and a black face peered out. The man said nothing, just stared at them questioningly.

"I am here to deliver a message from Governor Patrick Henry to Mr. Burwick, my good man," the lieutenant explained, "if you would be so good as to inform him of my presence."

The man shut the door in their faces, and they could hear his heavy footsteps moving away from them. In a few minutes, he was back, opening the door and inviting them in with a wordless gesture of one big hand. He was huge! He led them down a wide hallway to a doorway on the left.

Quickly, Sarah located Basil Burwick, seated behind a large desk with papers scattered across it. He rose when they entered, a scowl on his face.

"Get on with it!" he growled. "I'm a busy man."

The lieutenant handed him an envelope bearing the governor's seal in red wax. "Governor Henry hereby serves you with a summons to appear in court regarding the woman you claim to be your slave, Dulcie, the wife of Marcus, gardener to the governor," he said.

"I am well aware of who he is!" Burwick snarled. "The question is, what is he doing standing here in my study? And you, missy," he said to Sarah, "I've seen you before. You are the daughter of Ethan Armstrong, are you not?"

Sarah shook her head. "No, sir, I am not. I am the niece of Charity Armstrong, my mother's sister. My name is Sarah Moore."

He grunted. "Welcome to my humble abode, Miss Moore," he said sarcastically, with a slight bow. "To what do I owe this honor?"

"Marcus and this young lady seek your permission to see his wife, sir," the lieutenant explained politely.

Sarah's heart sank, as Burwick's lips curled into a sneer. He was going to refuse to let them see Dulcie! Please, Lord, help me persuade him! she prayed silently.

"She was so upset the night you . . . claimed her," she said as calmly as she could with the blood pounding through her veins the way it was. "I believe we can reassure her, calm her fears. I am sure she would be more useful to you then. And, of course, we want to comfort her." Where had those words come from? she thought in amazement. They sounded so reasonable! "Thank you, Lord!" she breathed.

Burwick, whom Sarah was sure had been on the verge of refusing, paused thoughtfully. Finally, he said, "You're right about the woman's condition. She's been in a real snit ever since that night, moaning and rocking and refusing to say a word, even to the other slaves. She's not fit for anything. If you can calm her down, it could save her from . . ." He stopped, looked at Sarah shrewdly, then at Marcus. "I'll let the two of you see her for a few minutes," he said instead.

"Samson!" he yelled, making Sarah jump. The huge black man who had opened the door came immediately into the room. "Take these people to the slave Dulcie," Burwick ordered, tossing him a set of keys. "And show them the way out when they are done."

As the lieutenant headed back to the carriage to wait, Sarah reached for Marcus's hand and followed Samson into the hallway and out the back door. He stopped before a small cabin with its door chained and padlocked. When he had the lock open, he motioned them inside.

It took a moment for Sarah's eyes to adjust to the dimness inside, for the cabin's one window was shuttered, and there was no lamp to give light. Gradually, she could see that the small room was furnished with a bare, narrow cot and a small table with one rickety-looking chair. The only storage space was on the mantel above the unlit fireplace, where a bowl, a spoon, and a tin cup sat.

Finally, she located Dulcie, sitting on a stool, wrapped in a dirty cover that Sarah thought must be from the bed. She was rocking back and forth on the uneven dirt floor, wailing that same wordless wail that had set everybody's nerves so on edge at the fort. The sound stopped abruptly when she saw them, and she grew perfectly still, her eyes watching them warily.

"Dulcie?" Marcus said softly. "It's me, sweetheart, Marcus."

She stared at him, and Sarah saw the blankness in her eyes replaced by fear. Then hope flickered in her dark eyes. "Marcus?" she whispered.

He went to her, knelt, and gathered her into his arms. Dulcie laid her head against his shoulder and began to sob, but the sound was much better than that eerie wailing, Sarah thought, swallowing the lump of tears in her own throat.

"Dulcie, if you've got anything of your own here, get it!" Marcus ordered suddenly. "We're going home!"

Sarah gasped. "Marcus, you can't do that! Burwick would have you both killed instantly!"

He turned to look at her, and the pain in his eyes was so intense that Sarah had to look away. "I can't leave her here, Miss Sarah!" he said, waving one hand at the squalid little room. "I just can't!" He pulled Dulcie to her feet, and urged her across the room.

Samson stepped into the doorway, blocking it with his body, his arms folded across his massive chest. Marcus stood staring at him, and Sarah could almost see his mind working at some way to get Dulcie past the big man. She knew he didn't have the chance of a snowball in July, but she also knew Marcus was going to try.

Sarah ran to Dulcie. "If we try to take you with us now, Dulcie," she whispered, "they will kill Marcus. Don't let him do this! The governor and Mr. Jefferson are getting you free papers. Please be patient! We will be back to get you as soon as the legal matters are settled."

Dulcie looked into her eyes for the first time. Sarah saw intelligence and understanding there, along with fear.

"I promise, Dulcie!" she said, holding her by both arms. "Do your work to please Burwick so he won't mistreat you or sell you before we can get you declared free! I promise we will be back for you. Soon!"

Dulcie nodded once, and relief shot through Sarah. She felt sure the woman understood. She reached up and whispered something in Marcus's ear. He turned from his contemplation of the man who barred their freedom to stare at his wife.

"Dulcie, I . . ."

"Go!" Dulcie ordered. "I wait." She gave him a quick hug, then a small shove away from her.

Sarah took Marcus by the hand and urged him gently toward the door. He stumbled after her, looking back over his shoulder at Dulcie until they were through the doorway and in the yard.

Suddenly, Marcus seemed to shrink into a frail old man. He began to sob, racking sobs that tore through his body and straight into Sarah's heart. But she led him on, across the yard, around the big house, and to the carriage that stood waiting at the door.

Sergeant Nelson took one look at Marcus and said, "I'll drive."

The lieutenant opened the carriage door, and got down to help Sarah and Marcus, but Marcus refused.

He pulled out a blue handkerchief and wiped his face. "I will ride up there where I belong," he said. "I'm perfectly capable of driving us home, sir," he said to the sergeant.

"Wait!" the lieutenant cried. "You won't be driving us anywhere in this carriage! Look here."

The sergeant climbed down, and he and Marcus looked under the carriage to where the lieutenant was pointing. The sergeant gave a low whistle.

"It must have been that snow-covered rut we hit back there," Marcus said. "It'll take some time to fix it."

"Too long for us to get this young lady home before dark," the lieutenant said, "as I promised her aunt I would do."

"Mrs. Armstrong will nail our hides to the barn door!" Sergeant Nelson said, shaking his head.

"Well, it can't be helped," Lieutenant Parke commented. "We'll have to seek shelter for the night, I suppose, and just face her wrath when we get home tomorrow. She'll be extremely worried all night, though."

"I could make it back on horseback," the sergeant offered. "I could tell Mrs. Armstrong what has happened and that her niece will be home as soon as we get it fixed tomorrow."

Sarah could stand the suspense no longer. "Will you please tell me what's going on?" she called from inside the carriage.

Marcus came to the window. "The front axle's cracked, Miss Sarah. We'd never make it home without it breaking completely in two. Then we'd be stranded out there on the road for the night."

"We'll have to ask shelter from Burwick," the lieutenant said reluctantly.

"Begging your pardon, sir," Marcus said, "but there are no ladies present in the Burwick household. I don't think Mrs. Armstrong would approve of Sarah spending the night here."

"Could we make it to Pleasantwood Plantation?" Sarah suggested. "It's just down the road a mile or so. My cousins and I took music and dancing lessons there for a while. Aunt Charity wouldn't mind me staying with the Woodards."

And so, after a slow and careful drive, Sarah found herself standing, again, before the big doors of Pleasantwood Plantation.

The Woodards were still in Philadelphia, according to the butler, where they were planning to spend the Christmas holidays.

"Of course," he added graciously, "in these circumstances, they would want me to extend to you the hospitality of the house. With the family away and Señor Alfredo not expected before bedtime, I'm afraid Mattie and I had not planned a supper fit for visitors, but you are welcome to share what we have."

The black woman who had given her a drink of water, showed Sarah to a room on the third floor, across the hall from the music room, and at the other end of the hall from Señor Alfredo's. She turned down the covers on the huge bed. Then she measured Sarah with her eyes, took a long, white nightgown from a drawer of the dresser, and laid it across the foot of the bed. Still without a word, she left the room, her footsteps as silent as she was. A few minutes later, she returned with a pitcher of warm water and set it in the basin on the washstand.

"Thank you," Sarah said with a grateful smile. Then, to make conversation, she added, "Have you been here at Pleasantwood long?"

The woman touched her lips with one finger and shook her head, which Sarah took to mean they should not speak. Had she done something wrong in trying to make conversation with the woman? But what was wrong with saying "thank you"? Aunt Charity would give her a lecture on manners if she didn't!

The woman opened her mouth and pointed to her tongue. Sarah gasped. Someone had made sure she could not speak by cutting out most of it!

By gestures, the woman made Sarah understand that, after she had washed up, supper would be waiting downstairs.

How awful! Sarah thought when she was left alone. Who would do such a thing? She was sure the Woodards would not treat a slave so cruelly.

Quickly, she washed her hands and face, tidied her hair, and hurried downstairs, hungry for some of the soup she caught a whiff of now and then—was it vegetable soup?—and determined to find out more about the poor woman without a tongue.

Sarah ran down the back stairs and into the kitchen, where she found Marcus seated at a big table. The silent woman was over by the fireplace, dipping soup into a bowl.

"Marcus, she has no tongue!" Sarah whispered. "Someone has cut it out!"

He nodded. "Mattie once belonged to Burwick, Miss Sarah," he whispered back. "She was a wonderful cook, but he claimed her talking got in the way of her working. So he put a stop to it. When Mr. Woodard heard of it, he bought her and brought her here to cook for his family. Now, you'd best get on in the dining room with the white folks, missy," he dismissed her, as Mattie set the bowl of soup and a small loaf of crusty bread before him.

The woman motioned for Sarah to follow, and led her through a long, dark dining room bigger than Aunt Charity's dining room and parlor put together! The Woodards must do a lot of entertaining, she thought, trying to count the dozens of chairs pushed under the massive table.

Mattie led her through a doorway into a smaller, cozier room, where Lieutenant Parke and Sergeant Nelson sat at a round table under a candlelit chandelier that sent flickering shadows across the room.

The butler pulled out a chair for her, and she took her place, wishing she could eat in the comfortable kitchen with Marcus instead. She looked around. The butler and Mattie both had left the room. She dipped her spoon into the soup and began to eat. The soup was almost as good as Ma's, she decided, dipping it up hungrily.

Suddenly, she remembered the special pot of soup Ma had made with the fresh vegetables from their first garden in Kentucky. How glad they had been to see the vegetables grow, to have something to eat besides game from the forest and the small amount of provisions they had brought with them from Miller's Forks! And how wonderful that first pot of soup had tasted!

A wave of homesickness hit Sarah. She wished she were back in Kentucky right now, with her family close around her, eating at the splintery table Pa had built and the Indians had chopped with their tomahawks the day they attacked the cabin and nearly killed Ma. But neither the table nor the cabin still existed, she thought sadly. The Indians had burned it last year while she was in Williamsburg. Ma, Pa, Luke, and Jamie had barely escaped with their lives, and little Elizabeth had been born in the cold, damp woods and had nearly died.

"They have an extra axle shaft in the stables," the sergeant broke into her thoughts, as he tore a piece of bread from the loaf before him. "The snow has stopped, and the overseer has agreed to let me borrow a horse so you can keep the governor's two to pull the carriage tomorrow," he added.

"Good!" the lieutenant said. "It shouldn't take long to repair the carriage, then, since we don't have to make an axle. Governor Henry can send over a replacement later."

The sergeant nodded. "This soup is good! Or maybe I'm just so hungry anything would taste good."

"Me, too," the lieutenant said with a laugh. "But this bread does seem especially tasty." He pulled off another hunk of the crusty loaf and began to dip it in his soup.

"Marcus says Mattie is an excellent cook," Sarah informed them. "She has no tongue, you know."

Both men stopped eating to stare at Sarah. "No tongue, you say?" the lieutenant asked.

Sarah shook her head. "Marcus says Burwick cut it out to keep her from wasting time while she worked. Mr. Woodard bought her then, and made her the cook at Pleasantwood," she explained, proud of her knowledge on the subject.

"No tongue!" the lieutenant repeated.

"That Burwick is a piece of work," the sergeant commented, his mouth half full of bread. He chewed and swallowed, then stood up. "I reckon I'd better be on the road to Williamsburg," he said, "if I'm going to get the message to

Mrs. Armstrong that Miss Sarah here is fine as frog hair!" He chuckled.

Sarah finished her soup and bread, drained her glass of milk, and set it down. "I am exhausted!" she said, covering a yawn with her hand. "If you gentlemen will excuse me, I believe I'll retire for the night."

"Good night, ma'am," the sergeant said, as he left the room.

"My room is just at this end of the second floor, ma'am, if you should need me," the lieutenant told her. "Otherwise, I'll see you in the morning."

"Thank you," she answered. "Good night."

Upstairs in her borrowed room, Sarah slipped on the long, soft gown Mattie had laid out, stretched and yawned, blew out the candle on the bedside table, and crawled under the heavy covers on the bed that surely was big enough to share, not only with Meggie, but with Tabitha and Abigail as well!

The fire flickered in the fireplace, burning low, casting shadowy pictures on the walls and ceiling. Sarah snuggled down into the featherbed and pulled the covers up over her ears and nose. It would be cold in the big room before morning, but the bed was warm and cozy, in spite of its size, she thought drowsily as she quickly fell asleep.

Sarah sat straight up in bed. Who was in the attic? The butler had indicated that only he and Mattie were in the house, though he hadn't actually said that. The footsteps were too heavy for the silent Mattie. She didn't remember the butler making much sound as he walked, either. Who could it be? Were there servants here that she had not seen?

Sarah eased out of bed, threw her cloak around her nightdress, and tiptoed to the door. She opened it quietly and peered into the hallway. There was no one there. She listened. The footsteps continued, moving over her head toward the other end of the hall.

She ran to the door to the back stairs, her bare feet merely whispering over the carpeted hallway. She grasped the doorknob and pulled the door open. The moonlight spilled through a small window onto the stairs, where a large black man stood, staring at her.

"Sam?" she gasped.

"Miss Sarah! What are you doing here?" He seemed as shocked to see her as she was to find him.

She explained about their mission to see Dulcie, and the broken carriage axle. "Sam, I thought you were hiding in the woods near Williamsburg! Have you been here all along? But why did you come so close to the man who was seeking to make you his slave again?"

He dropped his gaze to the floor. "I had, uh, duties here," he mumbled. "Anyway, I wanted to be near Ma," he added, again looking her in the eyes.

"The governor and Mr. Jefferson are working on getting you and your ma declared legally free," she assured him.

"You know Burwick cut out Mattie's tongue," he said.

She reached out to touch his arm. "I know, Sam, but Dulcie . . ."

"You know how she carries on when she's upset," he reminded her. "If he got tired of hearing it . . ."

"Your pa and I talked with her about obeying Burwick until she can be freed. She seemed to understand, Sam."

"Oh, she understands," he answered. "That awful wailing is just the way she grieves, half Indian, half islander."

"It will be all right, Sam," she tried to comfort him. "We will get her away from Burwick soon."

Suddenly, he smiled broadly. "Maybe sooner than you think, Miss Sarah," he said, turning toward the stairs.

She reached out an arm to stop him. "What do you mean, Sam? You're not planning anything foolish, are you? Marcus wanted to break her out of there today, but she and I together persuaded him to wait. Why, Burwick wouldn't hesitate to kill to keep what he thinks is his!"

"I know," he said calmly, taking a step down. Then he turned back to her. "Miss Sarah, if I don't see you again," he said seriously, his dark eyes boring into hers, "I want to thank you for all you've done—being so kind to Ma at Harrodstown, insisting that they rescue me from the Indians, being such a good friend to my pa and me."

A shiver traveled down Sarah's spine. Sam was planning something, something so dangerous that he thought he might not come back, might never see her again. "Sam, please don't . . . ," she began.

"Good-bye, Miss Sarah," he said, and he was down the stairs and through the door at the bottom before she could gather her wits.

Where was he going? Should she try to find Marcus and tell him what his son was about to do? But what was he about to do? Was he going to Wickland alone to try to get his mother? Surely he knew how hopeless that was!

Sarah ran to the small window and tried to see out, but it was too high for her. Quickly, she ran down the hallway to the tall windows in the ballroom.

The night was clear. Moonlight shone down coldly on the snow-covered grass that stretched below her and fell in a silver path across the dark river. Nothing moved, except a faint wind that stirred the naked branches of the big trees and whispered in the shrubbery. Sam was nowhere to be seen.

★ Chapter Nineteen ★

She hurried back to the hallway and all the way to its end, where a window looked out toward Wickland.

There was Sam! She could just make out his figure slipping from tree to tree like an Indian, definitely on his way to Burwick's plantation.

Sarah hurried back to her room and put on her clothes and her shoes and stockings. She picked up her cloak. She had to find Marcus and warn him about Sam! Maybe she should tell the lieutenant, as well, though she was afraid that even the three of them would be totally useless against Burwick's army of roughnecks and slaves.

She found Marcus sleeping in the attic. "Dear Lord, help us!" he breathed when she told him about Sam.

"I'm going to tell the lieutenant," she said. "Maybe he will know something we can do. I think we're too late to overtake Sam before he gets there."

"Miss Sarah . . . ," Marcus began, but she was already down the stairs and heading for Lieutenant Parke's room.

She knocked on the door she thought was his, and heard a man's voice answer gruffly, "What is it?"

Suddenly, she decided to test his knowledge of the anti-smuggling operation her uncle had headed. "John 3:19!" she said in a loud whisper.

She heard the creak of a bedstead, then scurrying sounds. "Darkness to light!" he answered through the closed door. Then the door opened, and the lieutenant peered around its edge.

"Miss Sarah!" he said in amazement. He shut the door quickly, and she heard more scurrying sounds. When he came back to the door, he was fully dressed.

"Do you know what you are saying?" he asked her seriously.

"I know that you gave the appropriate response to the code John 3:19," she answered. "My uncle was captured fighting against slave smuggling. I assume you are involved, too."

Señor Alfredo opened the door at the end of the stairway and came in, fully dressed.

"*¿Que ocurre?*" he asked. "What is going on?"

"Marcus's son is on his way to Wickland," Sarah explained. "I think he plans some drastic action to free his ma. It's too late to stop him, but he can't fight all Burwick's men alone. I don't even think the two of you and Marcus would make any difference. What can we do?"

" 'We' can do nothing!" Marcus said behind her. "You go back to bed, Miss Sarah. Facing Burwick's men would be nothing compared to your aunt's wrath if I let you even see what likely will happen tonight at Wickland!"

He turned to the militiaman and the Spaniard. "If you gentlemen are willing to help, we need to hurry. If you don't want to go, I will understand and go on my own."

Señor Alfredo turned and hurried from the hall, and Sarah heard his footsteps mounting the stairs.

The lieutenant went back into his room and came out

with his cloak. "Lead the way, my good man," he said to Marcus.

Señor Alfredo came back carrying a thin sword. "*¡Tengo que irme!*" he shouted in Spanish, something Sarah rarely had heard him use. Then he turned and looked her in the eyes. "I have to go!" he translated. He turned and ran down the back stairs after the lieutenant and Marcus.

Sarah knew it would do no good to beg them to let her go. Again, she ran to the end window, watching the three men as they made their way across the fields toward Wickland, Señor Alfredo running to keep up with the lieu-tenant's long strides and Marcus' eagerness.

How could she just go back to bed and to sleep, knowing that her friends were heading into almost certain death! She had to know what was happening!

Throwing her cloak around her, she ran down the back stairs. The butler was waiting for her at the foot.

"Can I help you, miss?" he asked, barring her way to the back door.

"John 3:19," she answered cautiously. If the Woodards frequently hid smuggled slaves, the butler must be aware of the whole operation.

"Darkness to light," he responded. "Now, tell me what's going on here?"

Quickly, she explained about Sam and the other men.

He nodded. "Sam could not stand knowing his mother was in Burwick's evil hands," he said. Then he looked at her, obviously dressed to go out. "But, ma'am, you don't want to be anywhere near that place tonight!"

"But, sir, I've got to know what happens!" she protested. "Marcus is my dearest friend in the whole world! And Dulcie and Sam are my friends, too. I can't just sit here, not knowing what is happening to them, and to Lieutenant Parke and Señor Alfredo!"

"Ma'am, I strongly suggest that you return to your room and pray for the safety of your friends," he said. "Now, if you will excuse me, I have work to do."

Sarah watched in astonishment as he slid the bolt home in the big back door, gave her an unreadable look, and disappeared into the kitchen area.

As soon as he was out of sight, Sarah slipped to the kitchen door, pushed it slightly open, and saw the dining room door swing shut behind him. Was he preparing to go calmly about his work polishing silver while her friends faced untold horrors? And what could he have to do at this time of night?

Well, she had plenty to do, she decided, going to the back door. She quietly slid the bolt back, pulled the heavy door open, and slipped outside. On the stoop, she looked around. The pale moon reflecting on the snowy ground lit the night like a thousand candles.

Sarah knew it was foolish to even think of trying to help with whatever was going on over at Wickland. She was small and had no weapons. But at least she had to get close enough to see what was happening to her friends.

As she had seen Sam do, she slipped from one large tree trunk to another, until she was at the low stone wall that marked the border of the neatly kept Woodard property. The field on the other side of the wall stretched away through tall grasses, rocks, and frozen weeds.

Sarah hesitated. Should she cross the wall and work her way closer to the buildings?

Suddenly, the sky lit up. She glanced quickly at the main house, but it sat dark and quiet, between her and the light.

Then, flames licked up through the light. They seemed to come from down near the slave quarters, where they had found Dulcie that afternoon.

Sarah was over the wall, across the field, and into the trees that bordered the yard before she knew it. She could hear the crackle and hiss of fire now, as more and more flames shot up into the night. She could see dark shapes, bent over, running here and there amid the flames. Where were her friends?

Lights came on in the big house. She could see figures outlined in the windows, then doors began to open and shut, and she could hear shouting and cursing.

What could she do? "Oh, Lord," she prayed, "please protect Marcus, Dulcie, and Sam. And the lieutenant and Señor Alfredo," she added, edging closer to the house, frustrated because she couldn't see around it. She needed to be behind it, where she could see down toward the quarters, where the action appeared to be taking place.

She ran to the corner of the big house and eased around it. At the next corner, she stopped and peered around it into the backyard. She located the path that led to the cabin where they had found Dulcie, but the cabin was engulfed in flames!

Sarah's breath caught on a sob, as she left the shelter of the house and ran toward the cabin, praying Dulcie was not still inside. But the door had been locked with a padlock. How could she have gotten out?

Suddenly, Marcus was beside her. "Miss Sarah, get out of here!" he ordered.

"But Dulcie! . . ."

"Here she is!" Sam said behind her. "Take her back to Pleasantwood. Mattie will take care of her." Then he was gone, back into the fire and smoke.

Suddenly, a gun went off from one of the windows above them. Sarah saw the bullet bury itself in a log of the first burning cabin just as a figure she thought was Sam ran past it.

Marcus had his arm around Dulcie, urging her toward the shelter of the big house. Sarah took her by the other arm, and the woman flinched with pain. She must have injuries, maybe burns. That was what Sam must have meant when he had said Mattie would take care of her.

They reached the corner of the big house and eased around it. No one was in sight. Marcus led them toward the trees, and behind the shelter of an outcropping of rock.

Sarah looked up to see the butler from Pleasantwood and several other black men jumping the wall and running toward Wickland.

"Take good care of her, Miss Sarah!" Marcus begged, placing Dulcie's hand in hers. Then, before they could protest, he was running back across the field. Dulcie sank down behind the rocks and began to cry, but it was not that eerie wailing.

Sarah knelt beside her, watching the smoke-shrouded nightmare before her. It was a scene surely straight out of the fiery pits of Satan, the flames leaping madly, figures milling around, running and screaming, yelling and cursing, all punctuated with gunshots.

Then she saw Señor Alfredo, dancing around like an imp before the flames, his sword flashing in the light of the fire as he fought a burly man brandishing the broad, heavy sword of a pirate.

Where was Basil Burwick, the devil's own? More importantly, where was Sam? Where was Marcus? What had happened to the lieutenant?

Suddenly, a wide tongue of flame shot up through the big house. Sarah heard more doors slamming, more yelling and cursing, punctuated by gunshots and screams.

Dulcie raised up and peered over the rocks. "Marcus? Sam?" she whimpered.

"I'm sure they're all right, Dulcie," Sarah comforted her, though she wasn't sure at all.

Violent cursing, followed by a loud scream, pierced her ears. Several men burst into the yard from the big house, pulling a struggling man with them.

"Let me go, you scoundrels!" he bellowed.

It must be Burwick himself. He had been caught by those he had so mistreated, some of them for years, and now he would pay the price. What would they do to him? Whatever it was, she was sure it would be horrible, and that they would make it last as long as they could. Sarah wanted to hide her eyes, but she couldn't. She had to know what happened to the evil man.

Someone drove a carriage into the yard, pulled by two horses that nickered and snorted their fear of the flames and plunged against the harness that held them. The men shoved Burwick into the carriage and three black men climbed in with him. Another climbed up to sit beside the driver. Was it Sam?

Renewed fighting broke out among those left. Burwick's men came running to try to rescue their leader, but the carriage pulled away from the house and down the driveway. Sarah could hear Burwick's yells and curses all the way to the main road.

She turned back to the house. It was totally engulfed in flames. Amid the flames and the smoke, the fighting continued, but it was not as fierce as it had been. Bodies lay on the ground, some moaning, some crying, some perfectly still.

Suddenly Marcus was beside them. "Are you all right?" he asked, bending over Dulcie.

Sarah saw that his left arm was covered in blood. "Oh, Marcus, you're hurt!" she blurted.

"A bullet went through my arm, Miss Sarah," he explained, "but it will be all right when we get the bleeding stopped. The fighting's about over. Let's get Dulcie to Pleasantwood."

"Where's Sam?" Dulcie asked, looking back over her shoulder at the fighting as Marcus led her toward the stone wall.

"He'll be along directly," Marcus said evasively.

"Is he all right, Marcus? Please tell me!" Dulcie begged, her voice rising toward panic.

"He's fine, Dulcie."

"He's with the carriage that took Burwick away, isn't he, Marcus?" Sarah said.

"Yes. It's all over now. Burwick will never harm us again, Dulcie. You are a free woman, but we will let Mr. Jefferson continue with his quest to secure legal papers stating that fact."

"What will they do with Burwick, Marcus?" Sarah asked. "Will they torture him? Will they kill him?"

"Miss Sarah, let's just say that Mr. Burwick is going for a little journey on one of his own slave-smuggling ships, with a lot of men he has greatly wronged. What will happen to him, only the good Lord knows!"

In the moonlight, Sarah could see that Marcus smiling.

Sarah never got back to bed that night. Once she and Mattie had doctored Marcus's bullet wound and tended to Dulcie's burned arm, a glimpse of herself in the mirror revealed soot and grime all over her. She could smell the acrid scent of smoke in her clothes.

Mattie had signaled to her that she could bathe and wash her hair in the kitchen near the water pump and the fireplace, so she would not have to carry the water up the stairs to her room. Silently, she had locked both doors so that Sarah would not be disturbed, and gone to work brushing and sponging the smoke and dirt the best she could from Sarah's clothes.

There was a knock at the back door just as Sarah finished dressing again. Mattie went to open it, and Lieutenant Parke and Señor Alfredo came into the kitchen.

The lieutenant had a sword wound over his right eye, but other than that, he was fine. Mattie treated the wound and tied a white rag around it, giving him a jaunty look with his shiny bald head and gray mustache.

Señor Alfredo's right shirt sleeve was slit from the shoulder to the cuff, and his long black hair swung freely about his shoulders for want of a ribbon to hold it. He sank down into a chair with a pleased grin. "*¡Ayye, vaya noche!*" he said. "What a night!"

The sun was coming over the horizon when Sam finally walked into the room and sank down on a bench beside the fireplace. He looked exhausted, but his grin was wide. "Well, Mattie," he said, "your tongue has been avenged."

Mattie grinned back at him and went on with her cooking. Sarah wanted to ask what had happened to Burwick, but Marcus shook his head at her and she said nothing.

Before long, they were all seated around the big kitchen table—Sarah, the lieutenant, Señor Alfredo, Sam, Marcus, and Dulcie—hungrily putting away Mattie's sausage, scrambled eggs, toast and jelly, as though they all had breakfast together every day.

The butler came in while they were eating, dressed in spotless green and gold livery! If Sarah hadn't seen him and his men plunging into the fight at Wickland last night, she would have thought he had spent the night snug in his bed at Pleasantwood.

"My black suit is ruined," he said, taking a chair at the table. "It's beyond mending, I'm afraid. So I had no choice but to wear my formal livery until I can replace it. But if slaves and soldiers and gentry can eat together in the kitchen like this, I don't guess it much matters what clothes we are wearing."

He turned to grin at Mattie, and Sarah saw her flash him a warm, special smile as she set a plate of food before him.

"You're absolutely right, Tudor," Marcus agreed. "I was telling Miss Sarah the other day that some day people won't care if black people and white people are friends."

Tudor! So that was his name! Sarah never had heard it, but it was good to know the names of your friends, she thought, and all of them who had been at Wickland last night would surely always be friends.

"Now, son," Marcus said sternly to Sam, "I want to hear all about how you organized a raid on the most wicked slaver in Virginia, where you got your men, and why you took it upon yourself to lead them."

Sam grinned at him. "Pa, I've been slipping over to Wickland for some time now, with Governor Henry's knowledge," he added hastily. "The governor wanted information, and I've used the language of the islands Ma taught me to communicate with the smuggled slaves. We have been planning this raid for some time."

"But you could have worked with Colonel Armstrong and me and the committee of freedom to stop the smuggling. We had even planned a raid for last night, but it was canceled at the last minute."

"Pa, I know your committee has been doing some good work, with its secret code and the raids it signaled on the slave smugglers. But just freeing the newly smuggled slaves would not cancel Burwick's claim on the others, like Ma here. No man in Virginia has ever treated slaves worse than Basil Burwick! He deserves anything those bitter men give him."

"I don't doubt that, son," Marcus said, "but it all seemed to come about so suddenly. One moment we were spending a peaceful evening at Pleasantwood, waiting for our carriage to be repaired, and the next everything had broken loose!"

174

"When he took Ma," Sam explained, "I knew I had to act quickly, before he sold her again." Sam threw a sassy smile at Dulcie, who sat clutching Marcus's hand as if she would never let it go. "Another day or two of that awful wailing, Ma, and Burwick probably would have cut out your tongue like Mattie's!"

Sarah glanced quickly at Mattie to see if she were offended, but she gave no sign that she had heard. She was looking at the butler as Tabitha looked at Seth Coler, or Abigail at Señor Alfredo.

Then the thought came to her that, with Burwick gone, Aunt Charity might let them resume their lessons with Señor Alfredo. What a Christmas present that would be for Abigail!

"Tudor and I planned the raid for Christmas Eve," Sam continued, "knowing Burwick and his men would be occupied with their drinking and gambling, and we could likely take them by surprise."

It was Christmas Day, Sarah remembered, suddenly overcome with longing to be back in the Armstrong house with her aunt and cousins, with the house smelling of wax and branches from the cedar tree out back, with Hester bustling about putting the last touches on Christmas dinner, with her Uncle Ethan sitting at the head of the table carving the goose or ham and placing slices on the flowered plates that once had belonged to her mother.

"When can we go home?" she asked in a small voice that betrayed the closeness of tears.

"Ma'am, we will be on our way in an hour or so," Lieutenant Parke assured her, getting up and heading for the back door.

Sarah was happy to find that he was right. They arrived at the Armstrong house just as Aunt Charity and the girls were returning from Christmas services at Bruton Parish Church. As soon as Sarah had satisfied her aunt that Sergeant Nelson had been telling the truth last night when he had assured her Sarah was all right, she went to bed. She didn't get up until supper time.

When Sarah went downstairs, before she entered the dining room, she saw that the others all were wearing the dresses they had worn to the Governor's Ball, dressed up for the holiday. Quickly, Sarah went back upstairs and put on the emerald green gown that would have had Luke telling her she had green cat's eyes, for sure.

She wondered what her family was doing this Christmas back in Kentucky. Were they celebrating the birth of their Savior in a new log cabin on Stoney Creek, with homemade gifts, and a dinner of whatever game Pa had been able to bring in from the woods? What she wouldn't give to see them all, to throw her arms around them and give them a big hug!

She went back downstairs, where her aunt and her cousins were gathered around the dining table, ready to begin their meal.

"We weren't going to wake you, Sarah," Aunt Charity said. "You seemed so exhausted! We waited to have our Christmas dinner at supper time, thinking you might awaken. Finally, we just decided Hester could save you some of everything."

Megan jumped up and came to give Sarah a hug. "I'm so glad you're back, Sarah!" she exclaimed. "I missed you terribly last night when I had to sleep by myself, with that old cedar tree out there moaning in the wind."

"I missed you, too, Meggie," Sarah answered, hugging her back. "And all of you," she added. "I couldn't wait to get

home!" She went around the table, giving each of them a hug.

Now, if only Uncle Ethan were here! she thought sadly, taking her place at the table as Aunt Charity picked up the knife and began to carve the goose. Where was her uncle tonight? Was he warm and safe in some Patriot home, enjoying a good dinner? Was he out in the woods trudging wearily toward home? Or was he, once again, shut up in some British prison? She refused to think of any other possibilities.

"I wish Pa was here!" Megan wailed suddenly. "He always carves the goose!" She jumped up from her seat and ran to bury her face in her mother's skirt.

Sarah swallowed a lump in her throat, and she knew that Tabitha and Abigail, and probably even Aunt Charity, were having a hard time keeping tears under control.

"There, there, dear," her mother crooned, smoothing the little girl's hair with her hand. "Your pa will be home soon, I am sure. He's probably having roast goose with some family not far from here, missing you just as much as you miss him."

"If he's not far from here, why doesn't he just come on home?" Megan asked, looking up into her mother's face with those brown eyes so like her father's, wiping tears away with the heel of her hand.

"Megan, if your father could get home right now, he would do everything in his power to do so," her mother answered. "You know how he loves being with you—with all of us—on Christmas."

If only there would be a knock at the door right now, Sarah thought, and we would find him standing there. But there was no knock, and Sarah sighed.

Aunt Charity gently persuaded Megan to take her seat. Then she carved and served the goose, and passed the steaming bowls of vegetables, relishes, and sauces she and Hester had prepared.

After they had eaten what they could, gathered the dishes, and carried them to the kitchen, they all trooped into the parlor. Abigail sat down at the harpsichord and began to play and sing, "While shepherds watched their flocks by night . . ." The rest of them joined in halfheartedly.

Sarah walked over to the front window and stood looking out, watching snowflakes swirl lazily around the light at the gate. "It's snowing again," she said over her shoulder, as Abigail began, "Joy to the world, the Lord is come!" The song seemed sadly out of place, Sarah thought, for there was little joy in the Armstrong household that night.

She supposed there was joy down in Raccoons Chase tonight, now that Marcus had Dulcie and Sam back home with him. She was happy about that, at least.

A man turned the corner onto Nicholson Street. Idly, Sarah watched as he plodded toward her, the wind whipping his shabby cloak about him and settling snow on his tri-cornered hat.

He stopped to lean wearily against the gatepost, looking up toward the house. Sarah supposed he was a beggar, and this being Christmas, she was sure her aunt would see that he had some supper. There was plenty left, she thought wryly, since none of them had had much appetite.

All at once, something about the man looked familiar, something about the way he held his head, and the way he reached for the gate latch. Sarah gasped. "Aunt Charity!" she cried weakly, but her voice was lost in the song behind her. She whirled around, ran to her aunt and grabbed her by both arms.

"He's home!" she cried. "Oh, Aunt Charity, he's home!" With that, she turned and ran for the front door, throwing it open wide.

Megan brushed past her and ran into the snow and her father's arms, with Tabitha close behind her.

Abigail came to the door, grumbling, "Where are you all going? I hadn't finished . . ." She stopped still in the doorway, letting the words die as she stared at the man with his arms around her sisters. Then she ran to join them.

"Thank You, God!" Sarah heard her aunt breathe, her voice catching on a sob. Then she, too, ran to throw herself into her husband's arms.

Sarah stood quietly on the stoop, not wanting to intrude, emotions flooding through her—loneliness for her own father, affection for her uncle, gratefulness that he was safe and back home.

He looked up and saw her standing there. "John 3:19, Sarah," he said, smiling. "Darkness must always flee before light. Good always triumphs over evil."

She smiled back at him. There was so much she wanted to share with him, all the events of the past few days.

"Welcome home, Uncle Ethan," she said. Then she added, "Merry Christmas!" for suddenly it was.

Echoes from the Past

As the winds of freedom blew through the American colonies, many colonists, like Sarah's Uncle Ethan, began to feel that a people who so eagerly sought freedom for themselves could not, in good conscience, deny freedom to other people. Such Virginia Patriots as Patrick Henry, Thomas Jefferson, and George Wythe (sounds like, "Smith"), along with John Adams of Masschusetts and others, began to speak out against the evils of slavery.

As the colonists' representatives struggled to write America's Declaration of Independence, the issue of slavery became a stumbling block. Representatives from the deep South, where great profits were made from slave labor on the cotton, tobacco, and sugar plantations, insisted that the institution of slavery be a part of the new United States of America.

John Adams was the respresentative from Massachusetts, where smaller farms and a colder climate made slave labor less profitable. He warned that, if slavery were allowed in the new country, in less than a hundred years their descendants would curse them for the troubles they would inherit.

In 1776, the words of the colonists' Declaration of Independence from England rang out:

We hold these truths to be self-evident: that all men are created equal; that they are endowed by their Creator with certain unalienable rights; that among these are life, liberty, and the pursuit of happiness.

It seemed clear that these freedoms applied to all people living in the new states. But soon people made the ridiculous claim that black people were not human, and, therefore, were not protected by this declaration or the laws that followed it.

Slave traders continued to capture the black people of Africa and the islands of the West Indies or buy them from enemy tribes. Then they brought them to America crammed into the stinking holds of ships like sardines in a can. Many died of disease or starvation and were thrown overboard on the journey. Those who survived were sold directly to plantation owners who put them to work in the fields, where they needed no special skills or the ability to speak English.

The price of a prime male slave averaged one hundred pounds before the Revolutionary War, but by 1779 had climbed to around one thousand pounds. (The pound was a British form of money used until the new country developed its own monetary system. It generally represented a sum higher than American dollars.) Virginia-born slaves were considered the most valuable because they grew up with proper work training and spoke English as their native language.

The horrible conditions on the slave ships and the cruel treatment some slaves received caused great bitterness to grow in the hearts of many slaves. Some continued to practice the "magic" of their religions from in the islands or Africa. It was not uncommon to find "voodoo" fetishes (homemade dolls), resembling their master, mistress, or a hated overseer, with pins stuck in them in an attempt to bring a "curse" upon them. Some took matters into their own hands and slipped poison into their owner's food, or attacked and killed their masters and their families as they slept, and burned their buildings. Some simply ran away, but if they were caught, they could be punished by death just the same as their fellow slaves who murdered their owners.

In 1778, Virginia passed a law that forbade the importation (bringing in) of slaves from Africa and the West Indies, or even from other parts of the United States, unless a slave owner moved to Virginia and brought his own slaves with him. Slaves still could be bought and sold, but only within Virginia.

The city of Williamsburg, though half of its population was black, never became a major slave-trading center. The city dwellers wanted slaves who were more sophisticated and better trained than the plantation field hands. Most of the slaves of Virginia's capital city spoke English well, and some could read and write. They mainly served as domestics—butlers, maids, nurses, cooks, seamstresses, coachmen, and gardeners. Some were apprenticed to craftsmen, where they learned to be carpenters, blacksmiths, stonemasons, shoemakers, barbers, tailors, harnessmakers, or coopers (makers of wooden barrels, tubs, and buckets).

Some slaves became such experts at their duties that they were made overseers of other workers, both in the shops and in the homes of Williamsburg. Some were so valued by their masters or mistresses that, at their owner's death, they inherited clothing, sums of money, or their freedom. Slaves were not allowed to own property, but free blacks, like Sarah's friend, Marcus, could and did.

Thomas Jefferson, though he owned slaves most of his life, fought for the right of Virginians to set their slaves free. George Wythe and Patrick Henry also believed that slavery was wrong, though Henry admitted that he owned slaves, because of "the general inconvenience of doing without them." Some people granted their slaves freedom through Last Wills and Testaments, though this was not legal at that time. Some freed all of their slaves, and others set free only those who had served them most faithfully.

In 1782, the voluntary freeing of slaves by their owners (manumission) was made legal in Virginia. Freed slaves were allowed to continue to live in Virginia. But former masters were responsible for freed blacks who were too old or too young to support themselves. Still, some Virginians objected to manumission because of the number of freed blacks roaming the countryside. The law was revised in 1805 to require that all freed slaves leave the state. Later, the entire law was revoked (done away with).

It was nearly the hundred years that John Adams had predicted before the issue of slavery was settled in America's terrible Civil War. This war separated the southern states from the northern part of the country and set father against son and brother against brother in a conflict that lasted for five years (1860-1865). Bitterness created by this war still is felt by some, especially in the South. Many blacks joined the northern army and fought to banish slavery from their land.

The current term, "African-American" was not in use in the late 1700s, when Sarah Moore walked the streets of Williamsburg. It did not accurately describe the "blacks" or

"Negroes" of that day, who often came from the islands of the West Indies and had never been near the coast of Africa. To call them all "African-Americans" would deny the rich cultural heritage of the islands that many inherited.

The black people of Williamsburg contributed much to the life of Virginia's capital city, as they attended to their chores, plied their crafts, and raised their families. They shopped in the stores along Duke of Glouster Street, as Sarah did. They attended Bruton Parish Church, sitting up in the north balcony, as Marcus did. They lived above the kitchens and carriage houses of their owners, or in small cottages in the section of town called "Raccoons Chase," where Marcus, Dulcie, and Sam lived. (Why do you think it was given the intriguing name of "Raccoons Chase"? Your speculations might make a good story for your next creative writing assignment.)

As the former colonists moved west, many skilled black craftsmen came with them to lend their talents to the creation of the new state of Kentucky. Sarah also helps establish this new state in Book Five of the Sarah's Journey series. *Shadows on Stoney Creek* is on sale now in your favorite bookstore.